"In the future, Andre Fuller chokes a woman to death while on drugs. He is brought to trial for his crime but the court instead of condemning him orders a less wasteful punishment: he must become the woman he killed. The struggle between the male psyche immured within a woman's' body and the female psyche that eventually emerges ... forces the audience to identify with the character's emotional upheaval. It depicts with painful accuracy how women are victimized in ... sexual encounters with men. One of the few believable portraits ... of what it feels like – sexually – to be a woman." Michael Perkins, *The Secret Record: The Story of Modern Erotic Literature*

"A special combination of science fiction and pornographic detail and rhetoric. The quality of the novel artistically justifies this radical strategy and invites association with other well-known pieces of science fiction that have employed it. Andre Fuller rape-murders Josette Kovacs under the influence of a hallucinogen. He is punished in a low-population future by having his brain put into his victim's body. His own body is given to someone else. He/she, as Celeste Fuller, begins an odyssey in which, after confusion and pain, Celeste makes a new and happy life as a woman and a wife. The story combines dramatic narrative and stream-of-consciousness in a tight control of point-of-view that vividly exposes the painful psychological transformation of Fuller from male to female. The shock to the male psyche directly experiencing the vulnerability of the female body is stunningly revealed." *20th Century Science Fiction Writers*

"Where science fiction is often male chauvinist this might raise male consciousness." *Worlds Beyond: A Critical History of Science Fiction*

"A good SF book and a rather better novel qua novel. Stine never offers an explicit sexual scene in standard cliché pornographical terms -- each one of his descriptions brings a personal and original observation into play. Many of these observations are not erotic -- they may even strike some readers as anti-erotic -- but they ring with truth. A genuine work of erotic realism, written far above the standards of pornography. The body of the novel lies in the male protagonist's response to biological and physical constraints and the transformation of his personality forced upon him by his female body. Effective ... rich ... rewarding...engrossing and unusual... littered with genuine insights." Ted White, editor, *Heavy Metal*

"What happens to a man's mind in a woman's body? Stine makes you inhabit that mind and slowly, imperceptibly, absorbs you into the existence of a woman until you as a man no longer exist. You become a woman, different from the one you raped and killed, and a better woman, at the end. Stine is a remarkable writer both for style, which is turgid with evocative detail and intense psychological insight, and for use of the second-person technique, which in fiction is used very infrequently, but which is required for the Punishment and Retribution parts in this book. There is eroticism in the book. The sex act is the most important sphere of life for this book, for Stine, for you, in the working out of the changes of psyche involved. ...and it is there that Stine takes you to show the subtle altering of man to woman in the body of Josette Kovacs, deceased. If four-letter words bother you, don't read this book. But then, perhaps you are precisely the person who *should* read it!" *Science Fiction Review*

"Passion, pain, real pluck ... a good eye for physical detail and a strong feeling for the human predicament." Fritz Leiber, *Fantastic*

SEASON OF THE WITCH

(with Filmography & Afterword)

Jean Marie Stine

Eros Editions
San Francisco CA
2011
A Renaissance E Books publication

This one is for Criss and Eden
In the hope that
Someday it might not
Be true

That dark princess
with suddening gest
she lowered her eyes of woe
and I felt the sigh
I wouldn't like to try
the changes she's going through
But I hope love comes right through
them all . . . with you.
                    — Donovan, "Season of the Witch"

On some as yet unspecified day in the future, really very close to now — in that limbo where nothing is changed and everything is a little unfamiliar — at the moment of twilight between today and tomorrow. . . .

PROLOGUE
Crime

There was nothing on the Formica-surfaced table top except coffee steaming from an earthenware mug and the illusion-thin reflection of a smile. The flesh smiled, the mouth and muscles and dimples at the cheeks smiled, stretching the skin tight into an open, masculine, confident, caring smile; but the eyes in the flesh were like dull onyx, hot and staring into the reflection trying to find an answer and finding only a freshly polished Formica table top with one steaming cup of coffee left by a forgotten waitress and a tissue-thin reflection of a face born with, cursed with, stamped with, but never, never blessed with a smile it had never felt, nor understood, nor earned, nor found a way of earning. It was not his, not real, but indelibly fused into sinew and flesh, so no waking moment could escape from it and no private, secret thought could exist apart from it. It was a smile given him unasked, and somehow accepted by all the chicks and broads and cunts as a real smile, a genuine smile, a part of him, because his smile and his face haunted some private dream of theirs, and they accepted it at face value as an answer to an ancient prayer, too exhausted by searching to question any farther, glorying in the smile and presence they had known would be there someday, since their hearts and souls were forged. His face, smiling, damning smiling, with eyes flawed and hot, stared back at him from its dream-thin reflection in the Formica table top, and he found the center of the trip engulfing him in acid-washed barriers of non-reality.

His hands were on his face, fingers moving with a serpentine sentience beyond his capacity to control, searching, feeling, touching, feather-light and hard, aching to know why this doughy flesh had been cursed with a smile that every girl loved and every girl gave to, gave herself and her love, trusting it to be something he could not even conceive or see or sense. But they believed in it with blood and heart until it was everything that had ever and could ever mean anything to them, and he gave to them, whatever it was they thought they wanted, receiving in return shelter and money but no comfort and no caring because they weren't reaching anything; there had never been anything to reach—only a tumescence too easily satisfied, so easily satisfied it had never had to develop into anything else, and so was nothing. But now he had to believe that whatever they wanted and whatever they were seeking was more than just his prick sliding into folds of flesh, even if their flesh—sliding in and out while they made something, some dream of their own out of his face and his smile and came to that, but never knew there wasn't any him there, and all their coming and their tearful, joyful orgasms that always seemed so profound and so much better than his paltry explosions of semen into protected wombs where the entire act was reduced to a sanitary moment of pleasure where he could find no further meaning—seemed now to be something more than he had ever seen before. And he had to believe, in the next-moment breathing-level, where even a reason for the rush of air to the lungs is inconceivable and imperative that they, fucking some dream myth of their own, com- pounded from his smile and his face and their excrement, believing him some heaven-sent, love-sent come, were reaching . . . reaching for something that was only an empty question he had never seen before now, in this Formica table-topped restaurant, trying to remember what he had done and why his face smiled while there was blood caked under his finger- nails and a stark cold fear in his gut more real than any empty dinner with its early-morning shiny polished reflections of despair, a reaching out to comprehend what that cursed smile had done earlier in the evening when some profound act of . . .

He flashed, white and cold and real, the acid beginnings of memory opening up his head and the Formica table top became a surface tilting . . . the floor opening under his feet, spilling him down through a sightless, soundless corridor where the gray blur of motion dazed his eyes. And he came to, steady and cold, the memory working its way up from the penis, seeking its womb, to his mind, and the whole celluloid

3

tape of the trip emptied into his mind like a left over movie from an eighty-cent theater, open-all-night, three-big-features. Three, seen over the loud snores of futility ground out by homeless men when he wasn't being kept and hadn't found a shack-up for the night yet. Only here it was and he watched it being replayed as the cops came for him through the Formica-polished sanctity of the restaurant.

And it all happened again—

again—

again—

again—

again—

again—

again—

"Here," the girl said (echoing in his mind). "Here," the girl said, her coral-lipsticked lips cemented together by exhaustion and sweat, the flesh pulling apart slowly so you could see the sticky skin curving away from the small opening until it reached the corner of her mouth and could go no farther. Last night those lips had closed over his prick, tongue sliding across his member with a motion so frantic it was almost an act of worship until he had come, white semen spurting into her throat, and she pulled away, spittle and sperm running down her cheeks, burying her face against his balls and chanting over and over in some convoluted mantra, "You're beautiful, you're beautiful."

But now her hand, instead of clenching like a fist on his foreskin, offered him a tiny pink pellet and he wondered why, for just a moment, in the California-matchwood cluttered interior of her apartment, he caught the odor of bitter almonds. But his hand closed around her smaller one and took the pill, holding it up to the light so it seemed to glow a pale rose from within, asking, "What is it?"

"MST," like acid and STP with a hypo of smack to juice it up."

His fingers held the capsule rock steady while she poured a glass of pre-canned, pre-digested orange juice from a yellow plastic pitcher and took the cap, breaking it in half so

4

the sand-fine pink granules fell floating on the liquid, inserting a finger slowly into the juice, careful not to break the surface tension, then swirling it about, sucking the powder into the orange undertow until it was gone. She handed him the glass first and he drank, tasting curiously to see if there were any immediate difference, even flavor, but it was only the sweet-sour tang of concentrated juice on his tongue. So he took it in two swift swallows, the cold biting his throat and stomach instantly, settling into an uneasy mixture in his gut.

He sank down on the couch which they had never really made up from the frantic fuckings of the night before when the sheets on the fold-out mattress were tangled and wet with a rich and heavy scent, handing her the glass with his prints oily and sharp on it, raised with the sweat of his fingers. Her hand wrapped around it with a strobe-light motion, a segmented folding that grasped the glass tightly, fingers slightly spread, and the other hand closing over it, interlocking, bringing the rim slowly to her parted lips where her tongue moved thirstily behind white teeth. She put it down on the dirt-ringed telephone stand next to the receiver taken off its hook and buzzing but not insistently enough to interrupt her lovemaking, and her eyes lifted to his, lonely, seeking eyes, lost in wonder at his face, her hand beginning to move over his body, through the tangled hair and along the lines of the musculature, coming slowly up to his face, to pull his head down so she could stare into his eyes and find . . . something; and he resisted, hiding the emptiness of his eyes, bending forward too smoothly and too abruptly for her to stop, putting his dry lips on her nipple, eyes hot and open, staring at the shadowed railing of her rib cage.

His breath whistled in and out, a loud throaty sound filling the silence of the plaster walled apartment, her nipple hardening under the wet lash of his tongue playing across the roughly surfaced tip, the fuzzy feel of down-like hair tickling his nose with each loud rushing breath sucked into and forced out of his body. Her hands groped over him, heavy and urgent, her eyes widening and widening until there was only an immense pupil inlaid in a milk-white and slimy stone, staring

5

beyond him while the deft, impelling motion of her fingers kneaded and caressed and coaxed, arousing a hard, cold need in his genitals that rose up, inching over her thigh, growing, swelling, climbing tree-tall, hard and steady. But his mouth still clung to her nipple, tongue flicking across the tip, eyes on her rib cage, watching, passive, as her flesh sank away, hidden beyond a vast kaleidoscope of color, the images wheeling and dissolving into patterns more stately than any human dance, fragmenting and breaking and re-emerging into twin colors that complemented and eternally fell through each other in a webbery macabre.

His prick rose up blindly, twitching, moving, finding its way down her body while his hands prepared the way, spreading her legs, spreading the wet, willing walls of her vagina, opening them wide, making them receptive as he slid the shaft of his flesh down, down, down endlessly into her, past every barrier, past every obstruction, seeking the core of her being he had never touched because she had never really looked at him, only at what she wanted to see, never touching him. He went in, slowly, slowly in, each single discreet movement an eternity, feeling the warm, wet smoothness of her cunt enfolding him, receiving him, taking his flesh into her flesh; and he pressed on, his hands clenched whitely on her shoulders, then working up to hold her face still, its wide, unseeing eyes looking into his while he pushed in and in, his body a knotted force, an agony yearning cruelly against her passive cunt.

Then her eyes came back to his face, while her flesh transmuted again into a sea of pale-hued color washing into and over him, twin colors falling endlessly through each other, and her eyes looked into his hot, real ones; and he groaned over and over again, his breath a half-moan whistling through his words, "Look at me, fuck you, damn you, look at me while you're fucking me. Fuck me, fuck *me*, not this stupid death's head smile that splits us apart no matter how tightly, fuckingly joined our guts are. Look at me, look at me, look at me . . . " repeated a thousand times in a pattern that tried to reach out beyond all their fuckings and make this one here, now, mean something to her, something to do with him, the him of the onyx hot eyes and not the unreal him of the foolish, cursed smile. And compelled by the power of his voice, her eyes came back to his, summoned out of her private dream to meet his, and suddenly, bolt uprightly terrified, seeing, her body twisted away, her cunt recoiling from the crying honesty of his prick trying to reach her through this fuck and make it mean something real to both of them. She screamed, her body revolting, and his hands clenched in the white sponge-rubber of her throat, cutting off the spewing forth of black fear that came multi-tentacled, writhing from her mouth, and went on, her face growing purple, twisted, eyes glassy, body limp, his come rising and rising, demanding to be free from his balls, blood spurting under the knife-edged sharpness of his nails, until his semen burst into her body, stuffing it, preserving it, filling it, finally, ultimately reaching her, leaving her quiet and satisfied in the aftermath of a gut-real fuck of honesty between them . . . between them . . . between them . . . sprokata . . . sprokata . . . . . . sprokata . . . The last flickerings of memory tape ran through the projector, its frayed end hitting sprokata, sprokata against the gears of his mind and around him, the black reflections of their helmets and uniforms filling the Formica-surfaced restaurant, were the man, the fuzz, the frigging cops, hauling him out from behind the table, spilling it and an earthenware mug of steaming coffee to the floor long before he could rise to surrender himself to their justice, twisting his arms up behind his back, the muscles wrenching across his shoulders while they crowded in from every side, pinning him in the closed walls of their hatred, hustling him from the building before the startled waitresses could put down their newspapers for a quick look.

He went passively, exhausted, empty, his semen gone, irrevocably committed to her body, his life gone, empty of all except an eternal smile and a death's head rictus settling in his veins where the blood of his body had tried to find a way to merge with hers and had found only death. A cold metallic surface touched his shoulder, stinging slightly, the abrasive roughness of the analyzer probing his chemistry, seeking the mechanics of madness as they emerged into the isolation of smog and street, its faint hum reducing his physical condition to a few symbols punched on a green tape.

They lifted his feet from the pavement, the night sky swinging into view as his head tilted back and his feet became horizon-level, and thrust him into the rear of their beetle-black, beetle-shaped van as other hands reached out and drew him in while still other hands moved around him, probing with sharp needles, and one of them, white cloaked, looked up into the goggles of the other, staring in at the reflection of his own goggles, and said, "MST, looks like," while bringing a round nozzle up to his arm, "this will bring him down," and triggered some remote and unseen switch, his arm stinging for a moment as they brought up still another nozzle saying, "and this one will immobilize him." Then they triggered the second drug and his body convulsed into a pain clenched nausea, throat opening in a silent gag that ended almost as it started, tongue and epiglottis a dead weight in his mouth, his whole body limp, the nausea still a fierce blade in his stomach but his muscles responding to no command, even the unvoiced, instinctive one of retching, toes and fingers, legs and arms, all motionless, and he cried for motion, no sound emerging, his mind frantic with strength and torn with fear.

But no movement came, only the van making its silent journey through the city while they computed and analyzed and decided, his fate fed out on unseen carrier waves to the computer beyond, running the maze of his life through on key-punched cards; one of the two men handling the printout, its long white tongue feeding through his hands and past his eyes, while the other brought out more instruments from the packed, neat, closed tomb-like interior of the truck, scraping the encrusted blood from beneath caked fingernails and dropping it bit by bit into liquid-filled beakers, watching the color changes and placing the final end product under a microscope, their images bent in the curving overhead mirror running the length of the van where his paralyzed eyes could see them and they could watch him from any angle.

"It's her blood. No doubt about it," the white-smocked doctor said, straightening up from the instruments, his face half-turning to the programmer before the computer board who fed the information into the satellite unit where it whirled a moment on the magnetic tracks of his tape and then flashed out to the central complex at police headquarters and back in an instant with the verdict. The programmer tore the final result from the outlet and nodded to the doctor. Light smeared across the black shield of the goggles, and they swung a metallic helmet from one wall and fitted it over his head until it covered all but the eyes and he could only stare up helplessly at the mirror, trying to guess what hid behind the dead professional mask of their faces, and a new machine lit up, a wide sheet of graph paper rolling through it beneath the black line of an inky indicator. "You are Andre Monkton Fuller?" the programmer asked, reading his sheet, eyes shifting to the graph across from him, working the paper forward mechanically a line at a time as he spoke, and the indicator swinging up and back as he paused, a spark of response to his own name running from Fuller through the head-set, down yards of circuitry to the detector. "Good. This truth detector having confirmed your identity, *this is your trial.*"

Fuller tried to answer, tried to speak, tried to move tongue and lips and throat, but only his thorax retained any life at all, his lungs still functioning shallowly, only enough oxygen to sustain consciousness reaching his blood stream, so he remained silent before their accusation, the tell-tale unrolling of the graph speaking for him. "Josette Kovacks, tonight at eleven o'clock, was found dead in her apartment on Alvarado Street by two interns sent when the Medicare—Life-Indicator at the base of her throat ceased functioning as her heart stopped beating and her name flashed on the emergency board at County General. According to testimony given by her neighbors, you had been staying with her for the last week—is this true?" The indicator swung up and back, leaving a heavy black curve instead of the even progression of its line. "I see it is. Very well, fingerprints found on a glass by the side of her sofa-bed proved, on comparison with those at the local

9

Selective Service Registration Office, to be yours. Further, the glass contained orange juice into which MST, a drug which it is illegal to manufacture, possess or take, had been mixed. The girl had been strangled and her throat lacerated in the process, the marks of fingernails in her flesh. Her blood type was found under your nails, and close analysis revealed it to have antibodies peculiar only to her chemical makeup. Did you strangle her?" A churning black fear, blacker than the sounds of hate from her throat or the purple-red of her blood, boiled in his chest, restrained only by the limp stillness of his body, and illuminated by multiple-screen, three-hundred-and-sixty-degree slow motion images of his prick and her cunt merging. His hand ached to reach down and unroot it, tear it out, rip it from his body and cast it away, never to be used again, to hurt him or anyone else, and in the overhead mirror his face smiled that open, confident, caring, masculine smile they all loved so much.

"Good. Having been tried and found guilty by the Division of Homicide of the Los Angeles City Department of Justice of the crime of murder, you are ordered to appear five days from today, on August twenty-third, before Judge Richard Goldstein of the Superior Court of the State of California, Division Eighteen. To that end I am empowered by the state to make certain you appear and hereby give authorization that a goad be implanted in your brain as provided for in the California Criminal Code, section eight hundred seventy-three, paragraph fourteen? He paused, licking his lips, the wet protuberance of his tongue distorting the narrow shape of his mouth and leaving the stubble of his beard glistening with saliva. "This judgment having been read to you, on this day of August eighteenth, you will be required to voluntarily sign a copy for the records stating that you have heard and understood it, in order to gain your release on recognizance."

The programmer raised his hand and the doctor lifted the helmet away, the graph stopping, its black line ending abruptly, the indicator leaving a Rorschach blot where the last of the ink fed from the tubing; and his scalp, damp with sweat, prickled, itching at the root of every hair, a maddening,

10

constant, fierce and agonizing itch that he could not relieve or complain of, but only lie motionless and fearful, waiting, as they came back again, with other instruments, sharp and glittering instruments that descended, spinning, against his head, slicing through the thin layer of scalp to grind, ratcheting at his skull, pain and blood blossoming, the pain sinking, needle-sharp, into his brain, the blood dripping like spring sap through his hair, and unconsciousness enveloping him, pain, itching, fear and all, only a sliver of his mind retaining awareness as they drilled through the skull and invaded his brain, raping deep into the gray, quivering jelly, leaving behind a tiny metallic flake that gleamed for a moment before the slow ooze of blood covered it.

The paralyzed shutter of his eye lay open, the green-flecked iris a narrow band circling the pupil, and the images sank in through aqueous and vitreous humors in the retina, trapped, held, and sorted, then fired with electron speed down the optic nerve to the brain, where, in a dim, half-recognized twilight, he watched them replace the top of his skull, cementing the bone into place and sewing his scalp together, leaving only a dark mat of blood in his hair to betray their entry.

His head ached and his arm stung and he reached over to rub the shoulder, his hand pausing in the air, the sweat-slick palm quivering faintly, a pulse beating across the ball of the thumb and the fingers moving slightly, trying to embrace the wonder of freedom as he lifted his head to see if it were really true, his body able to move, muscles able to expand and contract at will, sliding over the blood lubricated bones in a coordinated effort, and fell back, bright pain screaming in his skull. Their hands closed over his arms and legs, lifting him from the table, his agony-weakened head flopping back on his neck, beating and beating and beating with a stomach-souring venom that shattered thought and resistance as the doors opened and a cool draft of air blew in, a metallic, drying chill on his damp flesh.

They set him down gently, one of the black uniformed officers coming out of the cab, helmet flashing, reflecting the brilliance of the street lamps, nightstick hanging by his wrist, putting an arm under him to steady his spinning balance, while the doctor stood before them, lifting his goggles and peering at him through narrowed lids. "I've planted a small metal goad consisting of two terminals and a receiver, in your brain. One is in the hate center, the other in the pain center. The one in the pain center is operated by a unit at headquarters and will activate at ten a.m. on the twenty-third if you are not in court. The other will activate it too if you become violent enough to attack another person. Any rise in activity in the hate center changes the electro-chemical balance of the brain, triggering the goad, and will send you into great pain, a pain much worse than the pain you feel now. It will be a pain so severe you will have to reach the courthouse or die."

The tight ache pressed against his eyes, and he tried to blink away a mucous haze, the doctor a blurred image who thrust a pen in one hand and a paper before his face. "Sign this, it's your release." His fingers took the pen and his name seemed to boil out across the bottom of the paper in a chaotic black line while the doctor's words still echoed, ungrasped, in the night. "Good." The doctor raised his hand in a peculiar signal and said, "Here This will convince you."

The agony came from everywhere, blazing in every cell, catching fire and consuming him in a nightmare torment that dissolved his very soul and threw him to his knees, puking the acid content of his stomach on the pavement. "That ought to do it," the programmer called from inside, and the doctor climbed back into the truck, the doors swinging shut and the light dying, leaving him alone on the street in front of his apartment, his mouth filled with the bitter taste of bile.

PART ONE
Sentence

1.

She was a small girl with soft brown eyes and hair the muted brown of aged oak. The shadows from the bathroom light flowed over her amber flesh as she writhed and twisted beneath him. A thin dark cloak seemed to cover her breasts until her back arched under the insistent probing of his fingers, lifting a rigid nipple into the light. Her breasts were small and full, somehow in harmony with the wide, fertile lines of her hips. But her face was the treasure: bones delicate, the lines of character strong and gentle. She looked like a girl who would cry over every injured puppy and unhappy kid, then spin around blazing anger at the world that had hurt them.

"I love you," he said.

Her eyes kindled into a smile and she sighed, reaching out and pulling his lips down on hers. The softness of her mouth surprised him, he'd forgotten what this kind of girl was like. And her tongue was hesitant, almost questioning, as he held it down, filling her mouth, and kissed her firmly, easing to the side and moving his hand across the acetate smoothness of her belly. Her pubic hair was sparse and silky, his hand sliding through it, finding her moist and open, catching the clitoris between thumb and forefinger.

The breath went out of her in a jerk, her mouth twisting away, closed in an agony of pleasure. His tongue worked down along the curve of her neck and the hollow of her shoulder until he caught the erect nipple between his teeth, teasing it with short, hard strokes. A moan came from somewhere inside her, and he could feel its passage from her stomach through her throat. Her legs spread, lifting her slightly to him, his hand curving, the middle-finger sinking past the walls of her vagina into the let heat of her cunt. He rolled almost completely off her, their sweat-glued flesh coming apart with a sticky hiss. Only his mouth and hand still touched her, making her move urgently, tightly around him.

14

He had never consciously known what he was going to do, he had only felt its pressure h him since he'd met her, a day after the murder. It had never entered his mind, and if it had he could not have verbalized it. Nothing that was happening inside, where the cold uneasy feeling in his stomach was momentarily etched out by the turbulence between his legs, belonged in the world of free food and easy fucks he'd known. But it *was* there, locked carefully in his subconscious until now, when it through his instincts, giving every movement a purpose he could not even sense.

Not that there was any question of the verdict. He was guilty and they'd said it. Only sentence frightened him. The law gave many choices, and they could take any, even death. That one didn't worry him, though—no one ever got the death penalty any more, the courts were too civilized. It was the other possibilities that frightened him. They could give him life without the option of parole, or ship him off to an institution for the criminally insane, or force him to submit to drug therapy until his personality was altered beyond all recognition. Whatever they did, there wouldn't be any Andre Fuller left; he would end tomorrow and there would be nothing in the world to prove Andre Fuller had ever existed.

She had never known who he was, he had not wanted her to. He thought it was because she would be frightened of him if she found out and he didn't want his chances screwed up. And like all the other broads, she had fallen for him the moment she saw him. Then it had been like all his other affairs, pretending to like the things she liked and smiling when she smiled, until, at last, she was willing to open up her body and let him have her.

He took his hand away and ran it over her thigh and into the small of her back as she rolled over to him and pressed against his chest and legs, hiding her face in his shoulder, the wetness of her tears running down his arm. Her body trembled, she had been close to coming and he had stopped intentionally, leaving her hung-up so she wouldn't object, his fingers scraping down her back, making her sob with pleasure. Then he was on top of her again, his prick flopping between

15

them, trapped, hard, hot and eager across their bellies. Her hand came down to touch it while her mouth turned up to his, her tongue sliding over his lips and sucking his down into her throat. He held her like that, with one hand on her back and one on her breast as she played with his foreskin, the eruption of his sperm a molten pressure he would not release.

She pushed him away and bent down, lips and tongue swallowing his member and he grabbed her as it touched the back of her mouth, pulling her up and looking into the glow of her eyes. He raised himself away from the sweaty paleness of her body, flesh leaving flesh with a wet kiss of dampness. The agony of his erection was an overwhelming need to cleave her body and surround himself with the hunger of her desire until he burst her womb with his seed, filling her and leaving them both satisfied. He sat up and backed away on hands and knees, the outside of his calves brushing the inside of her sweat-dampened legs. Her arms came away from his sides and she lay a moment, looking up, the drifting light hiding her eyes in shadowy caverns. The silver crescents of her body, arc of thigh, arc of breast, arc of cheek, moved in the darkness of the bedroom, the darker patch of her pubic hair lost in the starlight.

For an instant his prick swung into the crack of her vagina, aching to let go. Her breath was hard and uneven, her body tense with the desire to save him in her; but the corridors of her body were unprotected, and her fear of pregnancy was even stronger, so she tried to roll away.

He caught her hips, holding her down, thumbs lying across the mat of her hair. She reached out to take his wrists, trying to pull them off. "Let me up, I've got to get the foam."

"Not yet."

Her face tilted up, the muscles above her nose knotted in irritation. "Why?"

"Foam tastes terrible."

"Oh," she said, her eyes going wide, then slowly and reluctantly closing as his hands caressed the underside of her hips, cupping the buttocks and lifting as her legs came up, hooking over his shoulders and he bent down, the satin skin of

16

her thighs pressing his ears. There is a point in a woman's body where the inner curve of the thigh reaches its fullest and folds back, narrowing into the pocket of the crotch; he set his mouth against it and sucked gently, stretching the flesh to a breast-like tautness, and his tongue darted over it, leaving it wet and bruised. The musky odor of her excitement filled his nostrils as he slid his mouth past the bordering fringe of hair into her cunt.

Her legs locked around his head, the soft flesh sealing his ears, and all he could hear was the rush of his blood and the throaty echo of his fear-tinged breath. His teeth scraped the straining tip of her clitoris, her body jerking and her legs tightening, bringing his face closer in to her body. The clitoris was a smooth, wet fold under his lips and he drew it in, teasing it with his tongue. Her whole body seemed to press itself against his face, as if she existed only in her thighs and crotch. His tongue worked farther into the slick-coated coppery taste of her vagina.

The reek of her body was all around him now, mouth and nose drenched in it as he breathed through them alternately, his lips still seeking the entrance of her womb. Then he found it, his tongue protruding into its pebble-finished tunnel, gathering the metallic sharpness of her juices and stretching farther and farther in. The walls of the vagina tightened, and he half-saw her fingers fumbling down, reaching for the pillar of his prick, and they brushed it, jerking a sob from his throat, and he buried his head deeper, nostrils flattened in the crack of her legs.

He clenched her buttocks until his nails dug into the flesh and held his face savagely into her, his mouth and tongue taking more and more. Her back arched and her legs clamped around his head until his ears seemed to split from the pressure. Then her hands fell limp and her thighs tightened convulsively, while her mouth opened in a soundless scream as her cunt slammed into his face and her body twisted in one final, awful movement.

He still held her to him, his mouth dripping with the richness of her release, bringing her back down slowly, her legs sliding from his shoulders, and she lay there, crying, dry-throated, her eyes wet with tears. He went down with her, hands spreading her legs as she eased away, and at the last second he moved forward, driven by a force he thought was sex, setting his lips on her cracked salty ones and sliding his prick into her openness. He hung there, knowing that he could wait and her mouth would eagerly receive his come, or longer until she had gotten the foam, but it seemed easier to thrust on and on, one continuous effort she did not even feel until his semen erupted, emptying into her body.

The plaster front of the apartments caught the flat crack of his steps, throwing it back into the rain-weary street, and he turned around briefly, hands thrust into the pockets of his jacket, the wind sharp on his face, staring at the ghostly shape of her building. Overhead smog choked the starless sky, settling quietly down over the city. He shook his head and went on, not quite sure why he'd stopped or where he was going.

He had eased out of the bed, letting his weight up a little at a time so the springs wouldn't creak, then stood finally at the head of the old four-poster by the discarded heap of his clothes. Her body was turned away from him, the face slack and pale in sleep, the corner of the mouth bent in the faint tension of a smile. She was curled in the beginnings of a fetal position, one wrist lying across her knees, the curve of her cheek shining faintly in the light. He slipped on shirt, trousers, jacket and boots quickly, stuffing socks and shorts in one pocket, and crossed to the door, moving silently on the carpet.

The heavy carvings of the bed rose massively amid the veneer-smooth, one-year-warranty matchwood furnishings of the apartment and she seemed utterly relaxed, a small, dark mound on the white softness of the sheets. She looked like the kind of girl who had babies easily, and it would be too bad if she became pregnant from tonight, but it really didn't make any difference, he wasn't going to see her again, not even if he wanted to. A quiet hum drifted from the heater as the

18

thermostat kicked on, stirring the air, and she shifted position, turning onto her stomach, one hand caught under her.

He closed the door and went out past the plaster-fronted anonymity of her building. His apartment was back the other way, high in a building very much like this one, but his stomach was cold, queasy, and he needed something to soothe it. There was a coffee shop a few blocks farther on, where he could sink down, lost in the booths, and relax. He brought his arm up, pulling the sleeve back, and looked at the luminous hands of his watch: only five hours left. Funny, the wind was cooler than it should be this time of year, and he held his arms tightly around his body, even though his jacket was fur-lined and warm.

He couldn't go back to his place, not with only five hours left until the trial. Anyway, his place was just like hers, crowded with cheap modern furniture that would still be there next year, without him, a little more run down and a little less expensive. He walked faster—the coffee shop shouldn't be too far ahead. The only real difference between her place and his or her place and all the others was that huge old bed. It was such an odd thing to find in the Southern California delicacy of the apartment, but he hadn't been surprised by it.

Now why was he thinking about that bed and that apartment . . . unless it was because they meant she had enough money to take care of a kid if she had one. She certainly wouldn't l get an abortion or give the child up; he'd found that out when he first met her. She loved children and while she didn't want one now, she would keep one if she had it. But she probably wouldn't have one, the odds were against it. A single, unprotected come wasn't enough to make her pregnant, so they didn't really have much to worry about.

Still . . . it was strange that anything had happened at all; he could usually hold it in and go on until they came half-a-dozen times and begged him to quit, but tonight it hadn't seemed worth the effort, and he'd just let go . . . what the hell, it didn't make any difference, there was nothing anyone could do to him now. Shit, he thought, and kicked out blindly at a dented ale can, sending it clattering, skittering down the street,

19

striking sparks from the pavement and rolling sideways down an incline into the drain. But maybe things wouldn't be as bad tomorrow as he imagined, they couldn't destroy his life over something like this, it didn't make sense. It wasn't intentionally his fault, he hadn't meant to hurt her, but how could he have known what would happen? She'd been the one who suggested the trip; he'd just gone along with her, trying to make her happy. Only now she wasn't happy, she was dead, and who should they blame? She hadn't cared what he was like when she went to bed with him, she'd just accepted his face without questioning any further. That made it at least partially her fault. If she had . . . had what?

What had he ever done besides take the easy way to what he wanted? There had always been willing arms and willing cunts and willing purses, all held out to him for the taking, and he had taken every time without fail, without resisting, without demanding any other effort from himself, without seeking any other way. And when she saw, when she saw him in those final moments, when she looked into his eyes and saw whatever was there, whatever he was, whatever had driven her to turn away in horror, in fear, and try to protect her body from the entry of his prick, try to force him out, keep him out and defend herself against the shaft of flesh and blood and gristle she found swollen within her vagina, moving with a power and purpose she had accepted until that glimpse of . . . whatever, he had choked her and ultimately killed her rather than give up that one hot spurt into her guts and try to face the truth he had wanted her to see.

He sighed and looked up, a faint mist sifting down his face and the city. Ahead the lights of the coffee shop glowed soft and warm, reflected off the polished tops of the tables inside, and reminding him of another coffee shop miles away and another night. He hugged his arms closer to his body and went toward it, stomach tight with fear.

2.

The court clerk rose, his flesh gray and lax under the dim light of the fluorescent tubes. "Everyone will please stand up," he recited in a toneless, rhythmless drawl. A door in the wall behind the judge's bench opened and as a tall, spare man with close-cropped thinning hair came out, the rustling stamp of the spectators rising honored him. "The Superior Court of the State of California, Division Eighteen, Judge Richard Goldstein presiding, will now come to order." They all sat back down except the prisoner standing in the dock, trying desperately to find the strength to move, legs stiff and tense, head aching with the exhaustion of too many hours spent drinking murky coffee and walking empty streets as morning came and sleep fled before him, a ghostly shade he could never quite reach.

Their faces pulsed in and out of focus, each beat of his heart dilating and contracting his irises and shaking his body with the force of the blood hurtling through his veins. They were all strangers, all unfamiliar, and if he had expected nothing else, the numbness of disappointment still clutched his stomach. No one he knew had come, none of the girls who had loved his smile, his face, and his prick, who had cried out to have him in them, to feel his penis sliding in the unfilled void of their wombs while his arms tightened around them and they sobbed in release against his chest, kissing him and pledging love, forever, undying love for him. He was alone now, caged in by waist-high metal bars and the blank eyes of the courtroom, truly alone, figures curled in the memory of death and mind dimmed by the black fear of punishment.

The judge set a thin attaché case on his desk and unlatched it, taking out a folder of papers and scanning through them, sliding the top sheet off and stacking it to one side as he finished each page, then picking up the bundle and joggling it back into order, the rap of the edges against the surface of the desk as short and hard as the sound of a gavel. "This court will now pass sentence in the matter of the State of California versus Andre Fuller, found guilty of the murder of Josette Kovacks while under the influence of an illegal drug, MST. The verdict has been reviewed by this court and approved; do you wish, under oath, and in the presence of a truth detector to enter any other plea? Silence being taken as no contest, this is your hearing for sentence. Do you wish to have a lawyer represent you?"

There was no point in demanding a lawyer; that would merely delay the outcome, not change it, and he could only hope they would have more mercy for him than he had been able to find for the girl. He hadn't wanted to hurt her, to kill her, to feel her flesh sink beneath his fingers, life fading with each unoxygenated beat of her heart; he had only wanted to reach her, to have her relate to him, to find . . . he closed his eyes, squeezing them violently together, red flashes seared behind his lids, and opened them, the judge a dark blot in the center of the room. "No, your honor. Except, I didn't mean to hurt her."

A current of air drifted across the room, stirring the cloth of his shirt and drying the sweat from his forehead. He looked into the waves of anxious faces, searching among disjointed noses, mouths, chins and necks for one familiar shape, but there were only the unfamiliar eyes of the curious fastened on his, hungry and waiting.

"All right," the judge said, his fist clenched on top of the folder, "is the prisoner, Andre Fuller, ready to hear the sentence of the court?"

"Yes, your honor."

The judge picked up the papers, holding them thoughtfully, the breeze rustling through them and folding them back in his hands. "This is the record of your life, an indolent and useless life, one that has offered this society nothing, and, to be honest, taken nothing from it. Except for the death of Josette Kovacks, there is nothing to indicate that you have ever been alive, and if we were to execute you—" his muscles went slack, and he grabbed the railing, supporting himself by his arms as the weakness of relief rushed in him, draining away the tension that had kept him on his feet for all these fear impregnated hours: this was not what they would have said if they were going to execute him "—no one would regret your death or notice you were gone."

The clerk coughed and the judge put the papers down, frowning over at him and taking a breath that swelled his body beneath the flowing judicial black. "But this nation has been through three crippling world wars and a plague that has left us with millions of dead. We cannot now afford an unnecessary death, and your death would be unnecessary, even futile. It would accomplish nothing, except to deprive us of yet another life when we need lives desperately."

An uneasy movement coiled out from the crowd, touching his nerves, the contact spreading to muscle and skin, shaking his arms as they held the railing, and his eyes met the judge's, wondering what they had in mind, the careful phrasing taking a strange and disturbing direction. "But you have taken a human life and you owe society a life in its place. Perhaps the real irony is that, had we found the girl earlier, we could have restored her life; revival techniques would have made it possible. But we didn't, and if we had, it would still have been difficult. She died from strangulation and the mind disintegrates when the oxygen is cut off from the lungs. Still, we might have saved her." The judge paused, his voice heavy, and lifted a jug of iced water, pouring a glass and wetting his lips with it. "Justice demands that you pay for her life with your own, *not* that you for it with your death. And we intend to exact payment."

Here it came, curving in at the last possible moment, the shape of their judgment in an ominous and growing form, rushing in from the unguessable workings of their minds and bearing down on him with a terrible speed that froze his eyes and left his armpits soaked with sweat. "Your body is to be given to society. There are men more important to us than you, men who have earned their right to live among us, but who have grown too old for a few new organs to save them. Their bodies are dying, and we cannot preserve them. We can preserve their minds, though, and their thoughts, and one of them will be given your body, his personality and his soul, transplanted to your brain."

The bitter taste of bile rose in his throat, pressing up from his stomach and burning in his mouth. His arms and knees gave and he sank slowly, slowly to the floor, the carpet slamming up to catch him with an elevator acceleration as the room disappeared in a gray swirling blight that dissolved walls and faces in a thick blend of fear, and the judge's voice reached him from beyond a membrane of cold terror, "But we will not deprive you of life, life is too precious for that. You will have your personality, all that is Andre Fuller, transferred to the body whose life you took, restoring life to it and balancing the scales of justice. Your life will replace hers, and you will live in her body. I can only hope you will use this life better than the one you had."

Fuller lay on the floor, hands clutching the metal railing, the chill bite of the bars his only hold on reality; the room spun and fell, throwing him into a void of gray-black light empty of everything except the icy support of the steel against his palm and the approaching forms of the guards, ready to execute the sentence.

Execute

execute

execute

execute

The cinemascope shutter-action of his eye-lids open on a pale cream overhead lighting panel brought him from a drifting semi-consciousness where his thoughts flowed together like the sides of a candle-castle to an instant awareness of the reality of the hospital walls around him, and he knew that the whole mad sequence of murder, trial, sentence was only the anesthetic reverie of some post-operative procedure he couldn't quite remember. He was curled on his side, his head twisted up at an angle looking at the ceiling, the smooth coolness of a sheet tangled under him, pulled tightly across the comer of his mouth, and he stretched, a lying in one position too long discomfort cramping his muscles, reaching over to pull the sheet down, his eyes flickering across the silvered

24

picture of a sleeping girl caught twisting uneasily hung on the opposite wall, his fingers circling around the linen, and brushing away a strand of hair plastered to his lips. The hair did not come free, but stretched back, out of sight, in a long, tense, glistening line to a needle-prick pain in his scalp, and he sat up, the sheet sliding down with a half-sensed rustle as the bed creaked under his weight, the girl in the mirror that was not a picture because their movements matched too, too perfectly, sitting up too, the sheet in the silvered depth of the reflection falling from her body, exposing two full breasts, brown-nippled, sagging slightly in a ski-slope curve and jerking with the abrupt intake of his breath. But it was the face that fascinated him, a familiar face, a face stamped by memory with a kaleidoscope of death and fear, the face of a dead woman. Fuller looked down past the tips of the breasts, erect with an excitement ignited by despair, through the cleavage, at the dark-haired, curly-thatched cunt, moving an unnaturally slender hand over the reality of breast and belly, touching, at last, the empty receptacle between the thighs. Then the finger went on, into the warm dryness of the vagina and out touching the egg-smoothness of the groin, along the slender lines of the legs, and back to cup the weighty mass of the breast, finally coming to the bones of an unfamiliar face—always desperately watching the image in the mirror reflect his every move.

He swiveled to the edge of the bed, stumbling, almost falling, catching his hand on the bedpost for balance, thrown off by feet that did not quite reach the floor and by an arm that almost missed its mark. Fear flamed through him, and he staggered to the mirror, gripping each side with strong beautiful hands, his head tugged back by the weight of waist-length brown hair, staring in at wide, startled blue eyes guarded by long, curving lashes, trying to gather the tattered cloak of delusion about him and find an exit from this drug-induced hallucination into the real world he knew must be around some disguised corner, some turning in his mind. But the blue iris stared back, feverish and intent, the surface of the eye shining with a conscious hatred, the delicate bones of the face outlined by flesh sunken with strain. He moved back, turning to the closet, throwing open the door, finding only a white hospital gown, closing it, not really sure why he'd opened it, then crossing to the bathroom door, looking inside and giving up. There was another door, and it had to lead outside, but he avoided it, even his glance ricocheting off it back to the delusion world of the mirror.

All his movements were wrong, subtly wrong, the length and timing and muscles different, different in strength and play and reach, and sweat ran down his flesh, matting the pubic hair into a pointed, twisted triangle, leaving the thighs damp and slick and cold. His mind churned restlessly against a problem too immense to solve, remembering clearly the feel of tumescent flesh engorged with blood and aching for the release of ejaculation, penetrating and thrusting and entering the yielding, open, hollow flesh of a woman. But now that yielding, open, hollow, usable, fillable, spread-apart and entered, quickly thrusting spurting and finished flesh was his, was Andre Fuller. And men would come, pricks hard, eager, long and round, demanding entry, filled with the desire to conquer and subdue, making their pleasure and giving it, ready to do anything to have it, just as every woman had desired the smile and face that had been Andre Fuller, wanting him to enter their bodies and bring them a pleasure they had only dreamed about. But now the face and the smile were gone, replaced by another object, desired, pursued, illusory.

Fuller wheeled, eyes fastened, clinging, to the mirror, hands touching the softness of his new body, a seed of resolve and direction flowering in his mind, remembering a phrase from the murky beginnings of his life, a chant of power, a mantra of dedication, and taking hope from it, grasped at the course of the future, clinging to the past, spanning both.

PART TWO
Punishment

1.

. . . you wake up when the alarm goes off into a numb gray depression, still clinging to the tattered edges of sleep, eyes closed, unwilling to face even the gloomy walls of the bedroom, muffled against the late morning sunlight by heavy curtains and air-tight windows, the hum of the air-conditioner working bone deep in a massage more relaxing than death. The pillow is soft and warm, bending your nose and flattening your eyes, shutting out the stark barenness of the hotel room, and, except for the imitating whine of the alarm, everything is so quiet it might still be sleep. Only it isn't, and your hand fumbles across the bed, crawling up the edge of the night stand, over the plastic lace pattern of the lamp dolly to the clock, pressing in on all the knobs until one clicks in and the sound dies abruptly and you sag back, face cushioned in the pillow, the pale, faded pattern of the wallpaper an oppressive image on the retina of your eye, trying not to remember that this is the last day and your time has almost run out, but knowing it in spite of your- self.

The rent has run out and the money in the purse on the other side of the lamp won't buy more than a good breakfast, the little you had managed to save having served only to get you through these few weeks, looking for someone to live with, someone with money, someone who will want this body, your body, enough to pay for it, not in cash but in future, and does that make you any better than a whore, and if it doesn't, were you ever anything else, or did it deserve a different name because you were selling, yes selling, for all that no one ever wrote out a purchase order on your prick, instead of a cunt? Or does the word mistress sound better, gentler, more respectable, like the word wife . . . wife? Andre Fuller, prick, stud, bought and sold, a wife . . . you shake your head and swing up, the soft fan of your hair swirling in front of your face, sticking to lips and eyelids, and you reach up, pulling it out of the way and

28

staring through curdled eyes at the half-open bathroom, taking warm shallow breaths, trying to reach some kind of decision, but not knowing about what.

You look down at your body, pale from too many weeks spent in restaurants and bars, waiting to be picked up and refusing every offer, promising yourself that tomorrow will be all right, but you need another day to adjust, to accept the strangeness that lurks, moment to moment, in everything, and you get off the bed, fumbling for the light switch, still four inches higher than arm level where it should be, and walk into the bathroom, the roughness of the worn carpet cutting into your bare feet, naked because you can't adjust to sleeping in smooth, silken, filmy things, and nothing else seems quite comfortable to this delicate flesh. At the door you turn and look back; there is an iron-red stain on the sheet, and you know it's time to change the saturated tampon, dreading the act, fearing the upset and the strangeness of inserting something into and taking something out of your body, disgusted by the intimacy and necessity of the cycle, though pissing and shitting have never bothered you, and almost unwilling to enter the bathroom and be committed, but remembering what it would mean if menstruation hadn't started, faced with the certainty that you would not have been able to survive that, going on in and opening the medicine cabinet, the puffy, disorganized mask of your face flashing by in the mirror.

Even the interior of the medicine cabinet is a strange land you have created, but never dared invade, filled with creams, and lipsticks, and eyeliner, and rouge, and powder, all alien but necessary to the charade of being a woman, easy to apply if you've been raised with them, but a carefully guarded rite no novice can master if you haven't. You reach in and take out the gray box of suppositories, pushing the inner carton forward far enough to work one loose, closing it and placing the tampon on top, balancing the container on the edge of the sink, and lean forward, the cold porcelain knifing into your belly, reaching down, searching for the string among a thick wet goo of matted hair and slick-walled vagina, finding it and pulling it out against a faint resistance, then flinging it into the waste can under the basin, the soft, disgusting splat tightening your stomach. The replacement slides in, forced up into your body, a few inches long, finger-thick, round and penislike, but there's no sexuality, only a necessity that must be satisfied, dampening the flow of blood with a hospital-white synthetic stopper expanding imperceptibly, filling with the excrement of menstruation as the doughy flesh of the prick fills and expands in the heat of excitation.

For a moment you stand looking down at your crotch past the rounded obstruction of your breasts, the chill edge of the sink brushing your hip, and the coarse pubic hair rough against your fingertips, studying the pinkish lips of the vagina and trying to believe that it's all real. Then you reach through the door and turn both handles, the water hissing out, splattering on the tile floor of the shower and drizzling against the translucent plastic panels, a dense, bellowing steam escaping into the room and condensing across the surface of the mirror with a pebble-gray finish that breaks your reflection into ten thousand distorted images. Your bare feet grate on the ceramic floor, slipping over the smooth steamy moisture, and the water crashes against your back, sluicing down your shoulders and dripping between the crack of your buttocks, a warm, nervous shudder quivering beneath your skin. The heat of the shower works its way over your flesh, easing, layer by layer, into the muscles, shoulders and body sagging, head drooping forward in a contented relaxation, long strands of hair molded to the sides of your breasts, a few curving across the flaccid tips of the nipples, and you sigh, sinking further into the liquid warmth, lifting a heavy arm to the sliver of hotel-soap, ripping the wrapper off, and spreading a trail of suds across your chest. The soap slides over your body, touching everything, even the places you don't want to touch, the water rinsing it away, inner-thighs and underarms and face, the leaden exhaustion of your mind crouched behind a screen of amber flesh.

Outside the cooler air raises goosebumps on stomach and arms, and water pours from your hair, a puddle forming under your feet and growing on the floor, rising between your toes as you step over to the basin, bending, the hair falling forward, and squeeze the water out, a few inches at a time, watching it half-fill the sink and drain slowly away. The thin cloth of the hotel towel is inadequate and your body is as damp as the towel, when you're through, so you wring it out and wrap it around your hair, keeping it from falling loose and the water from running down your back and you stare into the mirror, knowing you have a pretty face, but that it must be prettier and it must be today, opening the cabinet and closing it on the make-up you do not understand and don't have time to learn. Your face stares back at you, the eyes flat and dimmed, and there is only one thing you can really do with the food money, only one way out, and you close them a minute, turning away and going back into the bedroom to the closet.

You open the door, your eye veering off the tangled, accusing bed, the freeze-frame picture of what might be a man and a woman, seen looking down through the vee of her crotch at the immensity of a prick that will certainly rip her open, almost surfacing in your mind, but dissolving away before a closet partially filled with clothes, all ordered by mail, and none of them really fitting. You pull a green dress from the shelf, the fabric rough and thick between your fingers, and carry it over to the bed, laying it down and taking underwear from the small dresser by the night stand. This is the moment you dread, have dreaded since the first day, since the first morning, never growing used to it, never accepting it, always repulsed, sickened, and degraded each and every morning, lying in bed until the last moment, letting every possible moment of the day go by before getting up, but still having to face it and do it and live with it because it is what must be done and you will live with it and force yourself to do it and someday, maybe, come to accept it, if only because there is no other way and you must survive and it is the only way you can survive, and you will and must survive so that some day, some incredible day, on some incredible morning, you will be alive to find a way out; there was a way in and there has to be, has to be, a way out.

31

Beneath you the bed sinks a little, protesting, the springs creaking as they coil tighter, taking up your weight and distributing it, the cheeks of your ass spreading on the cool sheet, and you stretch your legs out, sure that you have the technique right at last, picking up the black acetate panties and wiggling into them. Then you roll the nylons up and draw them over your foot, adjusting heel and toe until they fit correctly, and draw them out, inch by inch, leaving a flesh-colored film over your leg that coats them in a tight, electric mesh which is somehow a part of your body and somehow separate, moving when you do but sensed differently, like an extra layer of flesh. The fabric clings tight to your leg, the elastic tops almost meeting, and you take the bra, having learned not to break your arms fastening it behind your back, but to fasten it at the waist, the snaps against your navel, and then turn it around, pulling the cups over your breasts and jockeying the harness up and down, from side to side, until it fits snugly, the inserts lifting your breasts and holding them in place. The dress almost falls on, with a whisper of smooth lining sliding over smooth skin, and hangs from your shoulders, the zipper rising easily up the front to the mid-point of your breasts and hanging, a glittering diamond pendant, from the vee.

Somehow the shoes aren't so bad, low heels are the style, and you can wear them without any trouble, slipping into them and going in to the mirror, unable to decide if the woman there looks all right or not, seeing only yourself, not liking it, but standing it, right now, this minute, today, and the next, for as long as you have to, standing it as you go back to the night stand, shove the money into your purse, remind yourself what has to be done, what must be done, and walk out, determined to do it, the

     knowledge
     a
     tight
     sickness
     carrying
     you

to
the
street.

There is something about two almost naked legs brushing together beneath the looseness of a skirt that is difficult to get used to; they should be slightly farther apart, separated by layers of cloth, instead of being close and open, the nylon-smoothness of the right thigh rubbing across the electric-smoothness of the left as you step onto the monorail, dropping the fare down through the transparent workings of the turnstile and take a seat near the rear, the flat tops of the buildings, a few feet below the level of the car window, accelerating past. Even with your head turbaned by a towel, leaning back against the plastic coolness of a neck-rest, angled slightly to stare out the window through the shiny reflection of your face, most of the male passengers have turned to look at you or shifted to catch a glimpse of your body out of the corner of their eye, thinking thoughts you know only too well and doing things to you in their minds, that, if they really want to do they can, for the right price.

You've tried, God knows, lying on the bed, sleepless, to imagine how it will be, their hands on your breasts, their mouth on your mouth, their tongue on your tongue, their penis coming into your body — your finger in your vagina a fantasy substitute already more real than you can stand, working in and out, in and out, the side of your thumb grinding against your clitoris, your finger a prick fucking the unfamiliar depths of your body, going faster and faster, frantically, until it jams in and holds, as if coming, but all you can do is lie there, breathing heavily, the sheets a little damp, and retch, quietly, flesh slick with sweat, mind dull and heavy, unable to find a single answer or see a single question. But that doesn't work, nothing does, you can't really imagine it and you don't really want to, even though it's real and will be more real, perhaps tonight, when you can find the right man and the right offer, and then you'll have to like it and have to accept it, because there is no other way.

Still they're looking at you or deliberately away from you, thinking, wondering what you look like undressed, what your breasts look like when the zipper down the front has been undone, the dress peeled off, and the bra removed, the breasts sagging into the smooth, round, flat-on-the-the-back shape all breasts take when a woman is on the bed and a man leans above her, reaching for the familiar, puckered brown of the nipples, breathing hard, the black tangle of the pubic hair over the pink lips of the cunt like all pubic hair, curly, rough and thick, the lips like all lips, slick, moist and ready, empty of a prick, but fillable, like any woman's. They've seen women naked before, most of them, they've seen many, but the unknown territory of your womb, the unknown territory of any womb, fascinates them, and they want to enter it, explore it, enjoy it, and leave it, for the next and the next and the next, until every womb has been explored, every vagina charted, every pleasure experienced and there are no more threats and no more challenges and no more mysteries.

The white marble towers of Wilshire edge above the roofs of the other buildings, expanding and growing as the monorail rushes toward them along its narrow track, whining faintly through the early afternoon air, and you stand up, missing for a moment the swinging weight of the scrotum, going to the back exit and waiting, one hand around a safety rail as the pressure of deceleration twists your heels from under you, throwing you off balance, and you stumble, falling to one knee, the hem of your dress riding up almost to the crotch. A tall, lanky young man with a deep tan and hair bleached by bottle or sun at the edges, rises from the seat next to you, the throat of his shirt gaping open, his chest thick and muscled, one hand closing tightly into the skin above your elbow and half-dragging you up, his body pressing into yours for a moment, firm and solid against your side, then moving away. You stare up at him, your eyes passing over the slightly bulging pocket at his crotch, seeing through it to the column, shaft, and color of his prick already unleashing itself for you with a, you know, never satisfied hunger, looking quickly across a chest and arms bigger and stronger than yours, to the wind-roughened flesh around his eyes, tightening as his mouth parts to speak, and the door hisses open behind you, a gust of hot wind hammering your back, and you gasp, drawing air into your lungs, and say, "Thank you," forcing the words past lips too tense to move, and turn away, abruptly, running down the steps, shoes clattering with dread, out of the station to the boulevard.

There should be a great many *salons* in this area, and there are, but the gleaming, polarized windows all say "by appointment only" and you still run, or it seems like running, past the smog-free, daily-washed fronts of a hundred offices, every step jarring into your rib cage, and only stopping, surprised, by a gilt-lettered sign that reads "no appointment necessary," the words whirling through your mind as you open the door and close it behind you, leaning against it, letting your eyes adjust to the dimness inside, the wide, mirror-tiled reception room like a cool, marble palace, the coral pale receptionist a fairy princess. You take a step for- ward, then another, the illusion vanishing like a film of soap trapped between two fingers, your reflection moving behind the gold traceries veining the tile, distorted by pockmarks and dirt, the tan carpet worn down in a line from the door to the receptionist's desk and from the desk to another door set in the far wall, and the receptionist a dull eyed woman with a face held tight by make-up and determination, her pores wide, plugged with flesh-colored powder.

"Yes," she says, looking up at you with just the crease of a frown over her nose, her lips closing firmly after the word is out. Your reflection is multiplied a million times in every wall, trapped in a mesh of gold lace, not the handsome, smiling face that lusted through endless nights of erection and conquest, but the wide-eyed, pale image of a medium-sized girl with full breasts, full hips and a thin waist that you see in every waking dream, starting up at night with a horror so thick it oozes from between your legs; and you force yourself to meet her stare, the answer coming out with a thin hesitance, a shallow breath bracketing each word. "I'd like my hair set, and my face done," your voice grates, but her eyes are still on yours, her hands still folded on the desk by her switchboard, and she must have some secret way of seeing through you with that dull stare, knowing you have a special reason for being here, and you go on, "I have a date tonight," but her face is still turned to yours, not moving, so she has seen the long silences for what they are and is sure you're not normal . . . "a special date," you end, almost sobbing as she reaches over and presses a lever, speaking and hearing a response drowned out by the roar of relief in your ears.

The door in the far wall opens, your reflection swinging away with it, and a plain woman wearing a gray smock comes out gesturing to you, and you follow her down a corridor studded with curtained recesses. She stops and pulls the draperies aside, letting you pass, and as you turn, says, "Change into that," pointing at a white hospital gown that brings back the momentary nausea of memory while she drops the curtain and disappears, leaving you alone in the hushed, narrow room.

A gleaming layer of plastic has been sprayed over the original walls, sinking into the cracks and depressions almost evenly, and only tiny discolorations mar the surface where use and age have eaten into it, and you look up at the fluorescent tubes buzzing below the ceiling, trying to remember how long ago they must have been in style: was it fifty years ago or eighty, or even less, you wonder, taking the robe from its hook and throwing it across the back of the contour chair where it hangs, limp from too many cleanings. The woman didn't say how much to take off and how much to leave on, she just accepted that you knew as all women know these things, but you aren't a woman and you don't know, and you can't decide, staring down at the swell of your bodice and thighs, what to do, though your fingers are automatically pulling the zipper down the back and sliding the dress from your shoulders, carefully hanging it up, then undoing the thirty-four "D" bra and folding it on one of the counters built into both sides of the stall. You take the thin material of the gown and drop it over your head and arms and it falls, held away from your body by the sagging roundness of your breasts, to your knees, a cool

36

draft of air moving under it, touching your bare stomach and acetate sheathed pudendum, the pressure easing the tension of your muscles, and you sink down in the chair, calves recoiling from the chill plastic, swinging back in it and closing your eyes . . .

. . . steps rap through the worn carpet, the plastic edge of heels, muffled slightly, striking the tiled, concrete surface, and your eyes open from the blank, self-directed darkness of thought on the muted light of the cell, the pupil narrowing like the shutter of a high speed, automatic camera, not quite finished when a woman, hair haloed by the brighter light of the corridor, enters, curtain swinging into place behind her, sealing you in cloistered privacy, her face hidden for an instant in shadow. She tosses her head to stare down at you, the wing of her hair flung away from the light and her face flooded with color, the shattering blue of her eyes gleaming like porphyry, her skin an iridescent tan, her lips small, rimmed with a pastel liner, slightly parted, the dark cavity of her mouth filled with the hint of tongue; and you look quickly down at your hands, the tightening in your groin familiar and unfamiliar, the muscles contracting, pulling in on themselves, the tension working through your chest, squeezing out your breath while a fever bums in your face, a patina of sweat soaking the material of the robe, staining the white a tarnished gray and dragging it against your breasts and hips, the outline of your panties showing through it, the dark patch of pubic hair embarrassingly clear. Her hip bones stretch her blue smock tight across the triangle of her stomach, the bulge of her cunt just barely visible, but easily imagined, the short black hairs curling over white skin, and lower, the pink lips and pink folds of the vagina, wet and lubricated, the entry easy, your prick sliding into the willing tubes of her body, the hot ecstasy of come only moments away, the luxury of the thrust a single pressure that holds and holds and holds, pressed to the very limits of her body, holding and holding, letting the excitement build with no effort but the strain of holding her; her breath screaming by your throat while one casual hand plays with her nipples, rolling their firm, excited points between your fingers,

37

until, with a never ending finality, it happens, the gasping, straining ejection of your seed into her body, searing through the channels of her womb, and finding, maybe, some ultimate rest. But in the slice of time, the thin, frozen-framed moment while her lips are still beginning to move, her tongue to quiver, and her throat to tremble, all you can feel is the empty, hollow contraction of your muscles, the dark, dank slick flesh of your vagina aware and wanting, not to fill but to be filled, not to enter but to be entered, the traitor of your body wanting what you do not want, needing what you do not need, and there is no way you can ever have this woman, ever hold her while she asks and demands and gets, her breath your breath, her need your triumph, her cry your victory, unless, unless . . .

. . . but unless is gone, the half-touched shape of the thought slithering away as her lips finally part and her tongue finally moves, and her throat finally says, "Yes, Miss—?" holding the hint of a question, waiting for you to answer, to fill the silence with a name, giving you the opportunity to speak, her eyes just a little intent, staring down at the band of your pan- ties showing through the robe, where, maybe, the lurching excitement in your vagina has somehow given you away, staining the fabric with the fluids of your body, and, not daring to look down, you say, "—uh, Fuller . . . Fuller," erasing the faint, questioning tilt of her eye- brows. She moves closer, her smock crinkling across breast and hip, looking down at you, reclined in the chair, body flat and open, and if she touches it, will you scream or gasp, wanting her, wanting any woman, but on your terms, and your terms can never be met again, so you kill the moment, fighting the words out, breathing deeply as they clog in your throat, and forming them one by one, "I . . . I have a. . . a date tonight . . . I'd like . . . my hair done . . . and . . . and my face made up . . ." there is a roaring torrent of air in your ear drums, howling through them, and she stands, still looking down, and you lick your lips, trying to find the right words to end it all, ". . . please?" not liking the plea in your voice, but unable to take it back.

The light flickers across her face as she walks around behind you and tilts the chair up slightly, going to one of the

38

cabinets and taking out scissors, combs, and other implements you can't quite see out of the comer of your eye, setting them all out on a tray that snaps into the back of your chair and beginning the long process of cutting, washing, setting, drying and combing with the words, "How would you like it done?" and at your shrug, going ahead, her fingers and comb tugging gently through your hair, teasing the scalp, relaxing as a summer breeze and you fall into a half doze, giving yourself up to her hands and pulling the blanket of sleep in protectively around you. Her hands move through your hair, cutting, snipping, the abrasive slash of metal on metal a rhythmic beat as soothing as the touch of her fingers or the taste of the breeze in the room, and you listen to the whisper of falling hair and the snip of the scissors, knowing there is nothing more you can do and not really caring.

"Big date tonight, huh?" she asks, her voice hushed. The lining of your throat is dry and sticky, chopping your answer to a gravelly smoothness, "Yeah, I hope so."

"I know how that goes, there's nothing like having a guy take you out and spend money on you to make a bad week better," she says, stretching your hair out with a comb and cutting through it. You can't be sure if she's trying to say what you want her to say, or if the thickness of your desperation is bending the sound and shape of her words into the pattern you want to hear, and if she is, really, what you would like her to be, would you feel any better holding her, the way you are now, or having her hold you, you wonder, sensing that the silence between statement and response is too long for each of you, bracketing every sentence with a half-guessed meaning, and you search for just the right phrases, not daring to be overt, but wanting to know. "Yeah, sometimes, if the guy isn't too bad."

"Oh they can be a drag, all right, especially the ones you don't like who want to go to bed with you and won't take no for an answer. But if you play your cards right you can get a good evening out of it all and not have to put across anything you don't want to."

39

There's nothing you can think of to say, but you don't want the conversation to die out, and you have to have time to decide whether she means as much as you can read into her words, or not, or if it's just your imagination twisting everything around. "Men can be real suckers."

"Yes they can, if you just remember to seem to promise them what they want, but that you can still act as surprised as hell when they want it, though that takes more work these days, and you have to do it carefully, so they don't realize they're being played. It's hard to find an excuse not to go to bed with them anymore."

A long time ago, in another universe, one of the chicks you were trying to make, and finally made, tried to hold you off and would have succeeded if you weren't always prepared, and her reason flashes, printed across the black and white memory photo of her face, and you repeat it, sadly, trying not to think what it would be like to meet her again, as a woman, and not be able to satisfy the desire to have her once more, "You could always say you were allergic to the pill and your doctor had you off it for a while."

She sighs, putting down the scissors and tilting the back of the chair down, away from your head, your hair falling free, and brings a basin of warm liquid up under it, slowly immersing it, a few drops running down the back of your neck. "Yeah, but if he has something, you're finished."

"Well . . ." you try to keep your voice even, not really wanting to say it, but having to say something, "you can always say it's your period."

"That won't stop some guys."

No it won't, you think, the split-screen image of the times you were too horny to wait and too lazy to pick-up a new girl and slowly, but carefully, aroused the girl you had until she let you in the blood-wet passages of her body and moaned that true heat moan while you ruined the sheets and found yourself as bloody as she and feeling, somehow, more triumphant; or let her tongue and lips and mouth be the recipient of your release, glorying in the frantic urgency of her head held down by the pressure of your hands; or once, once only, found your hands, your fingers slipping into the wet looseness of a rectum as your prick slid into the wet looseness of a cunt, and felt the rushing charge of your prick through the thin flesh between, and thought that, just this once, what would it be like, coming out and lifting her hips a little higher and screwing her in the ass until you both came, giving each other strange looks later, but never mentioning it. "No, it won't," you agree.

"My name's Gloria," she offers, but you can't think of your name, if you have a name, and let the silence drag on and on, wanting to leave the possibility open, but not wanting, now, to have anyone touch you or hold you or kiss you, but know that, maybe someday, you will and the need for a woman will be overpowering and you will need this woman, skilled in the kind of love you will need, and finally say, "We ought to get together for a drink, someday, Gloria," and give yourself up totally to the silence.

2.

The hot, denigrating, sun-blasted, blood-sucking outside air dies out in the re-processed, supercooled, cyclone darkness of the bar, vanishing as the last sliver of light is forever, undeniably, finally stoppered by the automatic, swingshut closing of the door behind you as you enter the rubber-plant and worn leather interior of the hotel bar, knowing that this is it, here and now, and if here and now fails there is no other way to turn or try to turn and that the men on the other side of the dazzling dimness that blinds your eyes had better notice, sit up and notice you and this, you hope, knockout body and, God, kissable face, and large, maybe, breasts, because if they, one of them, with their backs all to you, but faces reflected in the mirror behind the bar as they sit, not quite daring to watch the girl with the naked body and the shaved and gold-painted pubis dancing on the stage under the ever-shifting amoeba-light of the color organ occasionally flashing the briefest, pale glimpse of pink cunt in the uncertain light of the room, which is what they, each and every one, are here to see, but not admit to seeing, and they, God help you, are your hope, because if, somewhere under that counter, there isn't one swollen, hard dick wanting to be fucked and to fuck, then there is, nowhere, any hope for you. There is, here, near the boltable exit, a booth facing on the bar, and you move toward it, the nylon-sheathed length of your thigh pressing out the slight stretch fabric give of your dress and then falling back with the step that is like no other step, because here it is the first real presentation of you as a woman in a woman's body armored by a woman's armor, ready for a woman's duty, and you slide into the booth, inching around in it until you are in the middle, full-face toward the men sitting, watching the girl, drinks by their elbows or held limply in hands that want to hold something entirely different, but who, if they for one second will take their eyes off the, now, strobe-lit, inviolate, wish-fulfillment fantasy of the woman bending backward, her hair brushing the floor and her legs, spread apart for balance, wide open so they can see, in those brief, heartbeat flashes of light, the whole, desire driven mystery of her body clearly and sharply illuminated, knowing they can never have her or touch her, but can only sit there, dreaming of it, can see, where you are sitting, a woman, clothed, shadowed, all secrets kept, but touchable, leaning toward the full roundness of her breasts, lingeringly visible, reaching for a book of matches from the bowl on the table and then striking one so its flame bursts out in the ignition moment of greatest brightness and touching it to the tip of a joint of Acapulco Gold. But none of them, yet, notice, still lost in the imagination driven reverie of what a good piece of ass the dancer would make and how she would moan and thank them for it afterward and really enjoy being fucked by them and their fucking of her would, somehow, mean more to her than all the other professional, one time only, you're-a-good-piece-of-ass fucks, given her by all the other men who cannot, quite, be as good as you are or mean as much, even if she, herself, doesn't mean that much to you, but you will mean a great deal more to her than any other guy even, if she ever has one, her husband, and she will remember you, even lying in his arms, and wish you had come back if only once to do her again, and hoping for that chance which they can never hope to get, they notice nothing, yet, but watch every last grind and bump of ersatz sex until the lights finally go off.

You take a long, long hit off the joint, the mild, sweet, hash-soaked smoke filling your lungs until you can't hold anymore, and let it settle inside, escaping slowly through your lips, the snapdragon buzzing of the high rolling up into your brain, colors brightening, and the old, old tunes they are playing through the stereo-system beginning to become deeper and more profound, the loneliness of the piano an acute fear-statement of the you crouched here inside an alien, woman's body, unable to tell or reach anyone anymore as what you really, truly are, but only as a woman, or a woman's body, and desperately wanting, somehow, a way out, and you look back up at them through jewel eyes clouded by tears. But still no one

43

has looked away from the empty lightshow on the stage, except to lift their glasses or pass laughing, horny, dirty, smutty remarks to their companions, and you take your purse from the table top and drop it on the seat beside you, noticing how high your dress has ridden, tugging the hem down farther, and pressing your legs together, not wanting to expose the vulnerable entrance of your body to their gross imaginings, and hoping the waiter won't come too soon, not before someone else can come over and order your drinks for you, and pay for them, because you can't, not now after paying to be made-up as beautiful as, you can see in the mirror behind the bar, you are. Besides it might not be so bad to see just what it's like to have a man touch your breast; you have, after all, always wondered what a broad feels when you kiss her nipples and why she cries out so much.

You take another hit and lean back a little, your stomach rumbling an empty, frantic protest, the true, deep, disassociated, lumbering stone mushrooming in your skull and filling every cavity of bone and every convolution of brain, and your eyes focus back on the bar where almost everyone has shifted to face the counter and are staring down at their drinks except one man whose head is cocked farther back and is looking directly into the mirror and you cannot quite lift the immobile weight of your head to find out and can only slant your eyes up to meet his, afraid to know whether he is or is not really looking at you, and, suddenly, hoping he is not, even if your life desperately depends on it, but he is, your eyes meet, and you glance away, trying to make time, needing to make time, having to find time to think, and grind out your joint, taking your purse, snapping it open, and fumbling for another grassette. But he is, without any warning, or reason, up and walking toward you, something shining with a metallic glitter in his hand, and he is tall, much taller than you are, much taller than you were, and wide, heavy, solid, his body massive as stone in a black turtle-neck and severe silk collarless suit, his face stamped with that wheeler-dealer, always screw first because that's how you keep your edge, look, and you look up as far as his chest, but no higher, bringing the joint to your lips

44

and reaching for a match as he shoves his lighter under the tip of your grassette and snaps the butane flame on, searing the yellow paper a dark black as you breath in, almost unwillingly, by surprise, and the marijuana catches fire and is lit.

"Thanks," you say automatically, stoned numb, letting the solid bulk of all the weeks of planning and indecision and knowing what must happen rise up and blot out everything but the responses you have to give, turning off with utter finality every part of your head and extinguishing, even, as much as anyone can, that ultimate monastical cell of consciousness that always waits at the farthest back wall of everyone's brain watching and studying and evaluating and judging even when you are so consumed with the process of living there isn't any other awareness possible, and stretching your facial muscles into a smile, parting your lips as you take the joint out and hold it, forgotten, licking your lips with that slow, wouldn't-you-love-this-wrapped-around-your-prick movement that excites the spark of hope you want him to have and sets it burning in his eyes and smile.

His lips work silently in hesitation and the mask of his face freezes for a moment while he looks for the right approach, sure there must be one, not wanting to take the wrong one and be rejected, and says, "I don't want to . . . bug you, but . . . you look like you're either alone, or have been . . . stood up." And, now that the nitty-gritty approach has been made, you should, can, must be able to let it carry you along under the weight of its momentum, making just the right responses, and, maybe, just for the evening, convince the high echoing chambers of your head that you really are a woman and really want his big horny dick in you, making you come with a super-keen fine fuck, and if you are very, very good and play things just right, he will, one way or another, keep you or put you on to someone who will keep you, because that silk suit and turtle-neck must have set him back a very nice sum indeed.

"Right the second time, stood up," you answer and he looks comfortable, his face settling into a grin. "How about if I buy you a drink and a little talk and if that works out, we discuss plans for later?"

You shrug, deliberately lifting your breasts and letting them fall, and his eyes flick instantly away from the low-cut vee of your dress. "A drink . . . all right?"

"Good," he says, and slides into the booth on your left side, signaling the waiter, and you inch away from him, staring down at his crotch and trying to decide how big it is and whether you will be able to take it, aware that he, with his shorts and trousers, is well protected, but you, except for a thin flimsy pair of panties, are open and exposed so he can run his hand up into your crotch with nothing to stop him and almost nothing to hinder him. His wave catches the waiter's attention and you glance back up, finding his eyes on you and realizing with a thudding shock that he knows where you have been looking, and the barely perceptible parting of his lips is the wrong anticipation of thinking you want it from him, and if his goddamn hands ever touch you, you'll cream him, the smug, arrogant, cock-sucking son of a bitch, with his horny prick thinking the warmth flooding your face—God is that a blush— is only embarrassment at having your womanly desire for his big dick found, when it's really anger, anger, anger . . .

"What will you have?" he asks when the waiter arrives, inclining his head respectfully and holding a menu.

You want something strong and quick. "A Black Russian."

He turns to the waiter, arm propped on the table, gesturing with one hand. "A Black Russian for her, and a Vodka Collins for me, double strength," settling back in the booth and looking over at you, amiable and grinning as if you were the grooviest girl in the world, or might as well be, because as far as he's concerned, you are, and this should really turn you on, to be thought of so highly by so obviously cool a guy, and says, with machine-gun arrogance to really get you because he is so super cool he can get by all the really difficult stuff with such laughing ease, "What's your name, where do you come from, and what do you do?" and you stare at your roach, rolling it between the ball of your thumb and forefinger, the chopping notes of the piano still in its medley of really old classics, not actually having thought much about this and finding no easy answers, searching carefully for just the right words and phrases, but constantly mind-pulled by the leaping, ice-clear music, fitting each fact and phrase together to make him realize just what he can have and still not give anything away.

"Oh, I come from here and there. New York originally, I guess, but, like everyone else, I wanted to find out if Los Angeles was as groovy a place to live as they say. So I came here . . . a few weeks ago, and I like it."

He picks up the matchbook and fiddles with it, twisting the cover back and forth, and you take another hit off the joint, drawing the smoke down and down until there is no more room at all and another breath would burst your lungs, and hold it, while he drops the matches back on the table and clears his throat. "Most New Yorkers do, like it here. I was born in L. A. myself, but I've been most everywhere else, for one reason or another, and I always come back. New Yorkers are a strange lot, though. A lot of them come out here for a few weeks to see what it's like, then go back hating it, and then move out a year or so later."

You shrug. "Well, if I can stay here, I will."

"Why couldn't you?"

"Money," you smile, flicking your tongue out just past the edge of your teeth to wet the back of your underlip, watching him watch the gesture.

His eyes do not, actually, narrow, or his face harden, but there is the lightning swift rearrangement of calculation, the subtle tension of thought as he cautiously tries to decide if you are a common hooker, or something more. "That's always the problem, isn't it?"

"It seems that way with everybody." You incline your head, tilting it to one side and taking the very last hit of the cigarette before smashing it carefully in the ashtray.

"What do you do to stay alive?" he asks, the tone of his voice very flat and neutral, his eyes shifting across the room as if looking for the waiter.

If there are just the right words and just the right phrases for the two of you to use to find your way to the central meaning of what you each want from the other, this has to be

47

the critical turning point, telling him without committing yourself if he doesn't want it, and displaying a certain class and difficulty of attainment, and you reply, "I haven't found a position I like here, yet. I'm still looking."

The waiter emerges by the table, never having been hidden by crowd or darkness, but remaining unnoticed until he is suddenly there, placing the Black Russian before you and the Collins to the left of it, and is gone, instantly, vanished as if he had never existed, while you sip down the cool, bitter drink, hearing with acute intensity the old, smooth sixties sound of the music, waiting for a reply.

"My name's Howard . . . Howard Sladek."

Each discreet note of the piano rolls interminably through the bar, the dying echo of one underscoring for minutes the beginning of the next, and the bitter tang of the drink clogs throat and nostrils, tightening the muscles of your stomach, leaving a disgusting flavor on the roof of your mouth, like bile or semen as if the ejaculation of his question, catching you unprepared, for you had prepared only to be a woman, but not to be someone, and each answer is only the moment's desperate evasion of the fear damp and chill between your legs as you try to assemble a personality or a background he can believe, and the answer distills itself from the atmosphere with a relief as abrupt and quick as death. "Celeste," you say. "Celeste . . . Fuller," slowly, but steadily lifting the glass to your mouth and taking it all down in one smooth, lingering sip.

He finishes his drink and takes out a real tobacco cigarette, offering it with a flick of his wrist to you, and, when you shake your head, lighting it and drawing in on it until the red coals eats it halfway down, his eyes closed, head leaning against the back of the booth, sure from the easy, not quite grin, on his face that you are going to go to bed with him, and maybe more than once if he wants it and is willing to do the right things to get it, and you try to reamplify through the immensity of the high, buzzing stone in your body, the utter reality of being a woman, breasts and cunt and legs and arms and waist and hair and wanting, wanting his penis hard in you and his arms holding you and his lips on yours and his tongue in your mouth and him fucking you deep and fine until the wind is up and you want it, want it, want it, the echoing rush of your breath so loud that it is really that loud and he is looking at you, startled, then not startled and says, "Want to go someplace for dinner?"knowing if you do where you will both go afterward, and what you will do, and you nod, in acquiescence, letting him help you out of the booth, reaching up and taking his outstretched hand, your own only half its size, and pulling yourself up, the dress stretching with the movement of your legs, rising nearly to the tops of your nylons, and you tug it down, following him outside . . .

. . . the shiny black plastic hood of his car sinks abruptly in front of and behind you, the eighty mile an hour wind hurtled off the smooth bubble top screaming in keen agony, cold and wintery even in the fading sunset heat boiling through the smog stretching out of the city more than an hour along the sixteen lane track of the freeway, almost abandoned to the faster, simpler commuter cars running to the outlying towns like Bakersfield and San Diego, and you stare up at the dust stained sky through the transparent roof, back wedged between the edge of the bucket seat and the door, eyes shifting on to and off his face, avoiding him when he takes his eyes from the road long enough to give you a puzzled sideways glance, wondering why you are so silent, but not daring to intrude for fear of cooling his whole play, and waiting for you to speak, but the empty sponge in your chest has drained away all energy and caring, and if he were to stop and take you now, you would not resist, knowing that nothing can ever matter, this is the fate you have been condemned to and you cannot escape it, the gray waste borderland outside the freeway fence, unrolled mile after mile before the passive surface of your eyes, neither seen nor forgotten, recorded, but unnoticed.

"I think you'll like this restaurant," he says, no louder than the sigh of the air-conditioner, and you know, though you've never heard of it before, that to be this far out, no matter what else is involved, it must be very expensive and exclusive, very good and impressive, which is exactly what he wants it to be, and you squirm around in the seat, straightening out and

49

stretching your legs, crossing one angle over the other and kicking off your shoes, wiggling toes that have felt all day, too cramped, the sheen of your nylons disappearing in the darkness of the interior, while he goes on, "but I have to confess I come here mostly just because I like the drive," and looking out you have to admit it is a very pleasant drive, indeed, one you would enjoy driving, and wish you could, somehow, get him to let you drive back, and, if you are very, very nice to him, maybe you can.

"It's cool," you reply, pulling your purse from its resting spot between the seats where it prevents the accidental, oh so very accidental, brushing of his hand against your hip, and opening it, angling the top so enough light falls inside, searching among the stub of your check book, the keys, the identification papers proving you are a woman who is these many weeks dead, the spare box of tampons, and oh God, what if your period isn't over by now and you can't, or he won't, go to bed, you must know and it must be as soon as you get to the restaurant, you can go to the restroom and check, but there they are on the bottom, the last of your Golds, and you take one out, lighting it from the lighter on his dashboard, and drawing in, your hand falling down between the seats, where, if he wants to, he can take it and hold it a moment, so you can see, just to try it out, what that would feel like, dropping the purse into your lap, remembering all the times you made fun of other women and their purses, but now understanding the whole, insane trial of having to deal with one yourself.

His hand drifts down, the edge tentatively coming to rest on the back of your wrist and then, when you don't resist, sliding over it, the fingers so much longer than yours that if you didn't spread your own, his, cupping around yours, would easily cover them, but, instead, curl between and grip against your palm, holding it lightly, and you tighten your knuckles against his and he squeezes back, the pressure tight and secure, and you sigh, the rush of the wind past the car like the rush of the wind in the trees outside your parent's house when you were three, in Washington.

"Maybe I sounded a little flip," you begin abruptly, with no warning to yourself, just starting to talk, the words emerging from your mind in your voice with no existence between, all alien and strange, each one catching you un- prepared, and you listen, wondering what will come next, not knowing and afraid, "but I am, really, enjoying the ride, and I'm sure I'll like the restaurant, if you say so."

"I'm glad," he says, and you think, maybe, he really is.

"I don't know what was wrong with me earlier. I've felt bad all day, just end of the period depression I guess, but I think I'm coming out of it," and you find, listening and thinking, aware that something is happening, but not sure, at all, what, that you feel . . . lighter, and you are, smiling, watching the few trees and the fiat, desolate ground blur by, and his hand, holding yours, is not too bad, and things might, eventually, work out. "When I was younger, we lived up north, before the war, and we had blizzards, and the wind then, sounded like the wind outside, very much like that, howling and relentless. I don't know why, but I've been thinking of that, of most of my childhood, right now. There are so many things that were important to me when I was a kid, that I seen to have forgotten; mostly. Funny, isn't it?"

His breath snorts from his nostrils and he frowns, glancing at your reflection in the left-hand mirror, then back at the road as the green rectangular suddenness of an exit warning slams by, unlit and unexpected in the gray-blue evening light, leaping forward and gone before you can read the white reflector tape of the letters, your eyes still vainly trying to grasp the image they've already lost, and he lets go of your hand, swinging the wheel sharply, banking the car across five lanes and roaring up the outlet ramp, accelerating as you emerge on a straight desert road, plunging toward the faint light lights of a town a half-mile below, his hands steady as the wind, screaming across the flat plains, tears at the hood and body, and your bare feet braced on the floorboards can feel the frame of the car twisting, caught between the arrow-straight speed and the momentum of the sky. His eyes are on the road, and nothing else, as the three story bulk of the town levels out ahead, but he is, obviously, eyes and mouth and tightness of the hands, thinking, his face set, immobile, and speaks, slowly, trying to speak, think, and drive as the red band of the speedometer passes a hundred and fifty, "I guess everyone does that, eventually. Something sets you off, a fragment of memory, a song, anything, and you begin to remember. I don't know why people change so much, it could be just maturity, or maybe it's a sellout. Who knows?"

His foot presses in on the brake as he begins to downshift through fourth to third, the yellow house lights of the suburbs jumping past, their speed-blurred windows taking shape and the dark thatch of the square blacker than the last moments of twilight as you pull up before the bright facade of a canopied building, switching off the engine, one of the doormen hurrying forward, silver braid flashing on his collar and down the front of his suit, while you slip back into your shoes and snap your purse shut, sliding the strap over a shoulder, waiting because he sits, staring forward, out of the window, down the empty street, breathing faintly, then shaking his head and saying, "You know . . and shakes his head again, "no . . . that's stupid."

"What?" you ask, leaning toward him, the fabric of your dress pulled tight across your shoulders, making it impossible to move an inch farther unless you shift positions a little, and the heaviness of his face is so brittle any sound may shatter it, so you reach out, his eyes focused blindly, glittering, the pocket of flesh above his nose knotted, as the doorman begins to bend, his hand reaching for the handle, your fingers not really daring to touch the back of his wrist, but held there, resting against the black hairs curling across his skin, wishing you knew what you had gotten into and with whom and why, but not knowing and only waiting, listening for the words moving behind the pressed-together, will-not-speak-for-fear-of-saying-too-much determination of his mouth, watching silently as his lips open, the muscles of the cheeks sinking, his lower lip drawn down to the edge of his teeth and the first throaty beginnings of a word cut off sharply and irreplaceably by the mechanical flick of the doorman's wrist pushing in and pulling out on the handle of

52

the door, dragging it open with a smooth professional step that brings him to full attention at the end of its swing, but you have never taken your eyes from those lips and watch the face around it, tissue by tissue, form itself into a limp construction of flesh and muscle, saying, almost as if in the continuation of the very first beginning sound, but ever so slightly changed in pitch and intonation, "No . . . not now. Maybe later, after dinner. We']l see," meaning, if I'm ever in the mood again, his own hand opening his door and getting out, so you have to twist around, one foot on the floorboard, taking the doorman's arm, and pull yourself up, onto the sidewalk.

Through the leaded windows, dim with reflected images, the pale ghost stars shimmer as the waiter leads you through the subdued clatter of the dining room, threading his way among the scattered growths of circular tables where too many men in dark maroon business suits are sitting across from too many lacquered, polished girls with mask-tight faces, all poised and just a little too attentive, leaning forward, eyes, attention, and cunts focused on their dates, and nowhere in the whole expanse of the restaurant is there the kind of woman who is a wife, unless she is one of the new graduates who has not yet had time to finish the evolution from mistress to the more enviable position of cheated-on wife and the financial security of being lied to, and you take your seat next to the cool glass panes, folding into the chair, but not quite catching it at the right angle, coming down on the edge, because, never, never before, has anyone pulled one out for you, and you smile, trying to pass over it, sliding back into the seat and taking the parchment menu in both hands. Over the top of the menu you can study, without being noticed, his face, the hair curling along his forehead and the narrowed lids of his eyes moving in barely perceptible sweeps across the page, all the puckered flesh at the corners seamed, blistered, the smooth skin between his eyebrows slightly pulled in, and a sharp needle stubble of the morning's shave beginning to darken his chin and throat, but none of this means anything for each and every line and plane and drop of sweat has been repeated a million million times in a million million faces until not even the combinations are original, but only ancient varieties of the same expressions and even the reasons for each gleam of eye and curve of mouth and blood-tint of skin are only variations of familiar patterns, but what pattern is behind his face, what thoughts and plans and desires are grinding behind the interface of his skull in the gray housing of his brain where five billion impulses flare every second and the true deep purpose of his bringing you here and almost, but not quite, saying something you think, but don't really know and can't be sure, is different from anything you can imagine or could have expected him to say, is hidden, and his words, whatever those words might be, are only the things he wants you to hear or will want you to hear, and you will never, beyond your own desires, have any way to know if they are really what he thinks, and will have to decide a decision based on what you hope you know and what you want to think, if he ever gets around to saying anything at all. The embossed gold lettering crawling across the heavy paper writhes in a black defiance and you can't quite make sense of any of the words even though they are all familiar, English, everyday but cheaper names that you have rarely ever seen in such a gilt-edged procession only once that you can remember when one of the super wealthy lays took you out to dinner to, really, show you off to her set and impress them with the stud she had attracted, even at forty-five, though they all knew how she had attracted it, because, sitting across from all those middle-aged, bored, and well bribed women like these here tonight, were countless other young, handsome, smiling young men, as these girls, and you, are young, pretty, and smiling, sitting across from all these middle-aged men, and full circle, you, in both identities have sat, always, below the salt, with those who are used, kept, and discarded, and been content to sit there, but now, trying to plunge through the fleshy barrier of his face to his real thoughts, wish there were another way to live, another way to do things, any other way to do things so you won't have to endure another thousand days like this and like all the thousands of days before.

"About nine and a half dollars for your thoughts," his words smash into the juggernaut of your thoughts ramming it back into your chest and bringing you to a thudding halt, breath ragged and blood pumping furiously in the stoned shock of being hurled back to reality and seeing his eyes as intent on yours as yours were on him, wondering how long he has been watching you.

"Oh, it was nothing, really," you say, closing the menu and laying it down, stalling until you have found a way to face him, hoping you aren't as transparent and vulnerable as you feel, taking the napkin from the table and smoothing it on your lap, then finding his eyes furrowed in concentration, trying, perhaps, to discover what you are thinking, as strongly as you are trying to discover what he is thinking, the two of you revolving about a common center, endlessly trying to decide what can never be known.

"I doubt that," he insists. "You were thinking very heavily, very heavily."

But the answer is in your mouth and out before you can realize its perfection, and you smile, in its wake, watching his reaction. "I was just wondering what it was you were going to say in the car."

The mask builds up in layers under his skin, never seeming to thicken or distort his face, but forming an iron-hard protection no one could break through. "Oh, that," he shrugs, an elaborate movement of his shoulders under his jacket as artificial as the come-hither look of an audioanimatronic robot in the window of a department store. "It was nothing, really. Besides, I'll tell you later," and you know, from the hard glare of light in his eyes, that if you are ever to End out, you'll have to force it from him line by line.

"Do you really expect me to believe that?"

His smile turns as bitter as ice. "It doesn't matter, does it? I'll tell you what I want to tell you. You have to live with that." But behind his smile, there is, you're sure, something else, something you can sense in the sharp lines around his mouth and the faint coating of sweat at his temples, something he is fighting to protect as you never fought to protect anything in your life and never had anything worth protecting, and, maybe, it is the same thing you were struggling to understand on the night when you tried, desperately tried, to reach through to that girl, what was her name, and make her see you, the real you, whatever that you might have been and destroyed everything in the attempt, died and ascended, phoenix-like, from your body.

"Are you ready to order, sir?" the waiter asks, standing at your elbow and, you realize, in just an instant, not talking to you, but to your date who lifts his eyebrows waiting for your response, and you can only, not able to recall a single item of the menu, reply: "Whatever you're having is all right with me."

3.

"Celeste," his voice is softer, lower, no, not really, only the same even strength, but sounds, strangely, gentler, and you look up from the rum pudding: "Yes?" "What . . there is a momentary shadow of a spasm across his face, aborted before it can really be born, "what do you want out of life?" The words sink endlessly through the deep- stoned caverns of your mind, plunging out of sight and hearing into unreachable darknesses and you stare after them at the faint phosphorescence of their wake, turning each symbol and sound over, searching among them for some quick validity, some near relation to yourself, but they mean nothing, they have no connection with you; you are, here and now, aren't you, doing what you want to do, and what is there to want out of life that you haven't had and aren't going to have, unless there is some- thing more, that something you never really saw, but half-sensed, half-guessed on your final trip into murder when, hidden behind the surface of every human reality, you glimpsed that everyone you had fucked was trying to reach a something you had never before known was there, and the dim shape of a question flickered in your head, and you look into the flat mirrors of his eyes waiting, dead serious, for your answer and the weight of any lie you know is, oddly, greater than your strength, and you lift the truth up and out where it issues from your throat and echoes through the room, "I don't know. I never thought much about it. What is there, really, to want?"

The skin over his cheekbones seems to tighten, almost as if in pain, and he waits a moment, dragging in a long breath before answering, "You really mean that, don't you?"

"Yes," the word is heavy and exhausted, and you slump in the chair, setting your spoon on the edge of the saucer.

"Haven't you ever wanted to have a husband and kids?" He leans forward, his eyes circling around your face in ever tightening spirals.

"No," you answer truthfully.

"Most girls do."

You sigh and pick up the spoon again, bringing it to your mouth and sucking it clean while you wonder what he is after and why: "I'm not like most girls, Howard."

He shakes his head, ignoring the irrelevant. "I knew that when I first saw you in the mirror in the bar."

He knew, then, before he'd even spoken to you, from just looking, penetrating the reality of your disguise as, how many others must have discovered it.

"How?"

"How did I know?" there is a desperate mocking laughter in his voice and he is after something that is, to him, very big.

"Yes, how did you know?"

"Your face . . . your expression."

You must know to guard it more thoroughly in the future, if there is any way it can be guarded at all. "What about it?"

"Like, your face wasn't used. It seemed fresh, virginal. Virginal, mostly, I guess. You looked as innocent and virginal as a fourteen-year-old. You aren't a virgin, are you?"

"No," you rap the spoon against the plate. "I guess I'm not a virgin."

He hurries on, as if afraid to let a single moment pass on his way to, where. "It doesn't matter, I just noticed you, that's all, and sensed you were different."

"All right."

"But haven't you ever even thought about having any of those things, Celeste?"

"No," you answer, looking away from him, out at the sky, "I haven't."

"Well, then," he asks, but seems to be pleading for an answer. "What have you thought about?"

"I don't know, not much of anything."

He looks, not quite believing, at your body and face. "In all this time . . . not much of anything?

"In all this time."

He finishes his coffee and signals the waiter for more. "What do you like, what do you care about, what's important to you?"

And behind the fuck-first-or-get-fucked hardness seared and branded into his face, mocking laughter in his voice and he is after something that is, to him, very big. into ligament and muscle, you can see, glimpsed through the split second crack of his question, at the bottom of a fissure inhumanly deep, the fear and human desperation and need to be needed, that drive him and every fuck-first-or-be-fucked clockwork demon in this room, but it is here, to be seen for just the briefest moment of revelation, closer to the surface than in all the others, trying, driven, to escape, break loose, come out, shatter the robot casing and reach out for something, you can't know what, reaching for you, wanting, somehow, your help, unable to ask for it but reaching, all the same, from behind the iron walls of its imprisonment to you, and, breath trembling, chest as thin as tissue, brain revolving in the oiled high of your skull, you do not know what to say, and retreat, once again, into the safe, easy path of honesty.

"I don't know, I can't think of anything."

He pulls back, not moving, but drawing back into the recesses of his mind. "How can you say that?"

"Because," you answer with dead level seriousness, hoping to force him to believe you, "it's true."

"But didn't you ever care about anything?"

And with a wrench the seal across all the corridors of memory tears open and you stand, with the abrupt flooded clarity of sunlight emerging from a heavy cloud, in the center of a giant wheel, and each spoke of this many-spoked wheel, is the shaft down which a thousand memories can be seen, and it spins slowly past so that every day of your life moves before your eyes and you know what dreams and hopes and aspirations filled you on each and every one of them.

"Yes, I have cared about things."

"What?" he asks, ignoring the non-presence of the waiter pouring you both more coffee.

"My dog and my father," you answer, the whole ornate structure of your life stripped to its impoverished bones and the awful loneliness and friendlessness driven through your mind, raping it of every carefully erected façade and baring it to your unwilling gaze.

"That's all?"

You toss your head, the hair whipping your bare shoulders. "All I can remember."

"But what do you like to do?"

"When I was younger, I liked to fish. My father took me fishing."

"What about your mother?"

"She died when I was young. My step-mother was nice, but she and my father had kids of their own after they married, and . . . well, they were her kids."

"That's it?" `

"Just fishing. We used to go out in his boat and drift down the river, letting our lines trail out behind us, listening to the wind in the trees, I've always liked the sound of wind in the trees, and waiting for the fish to bite."

"What was important to you?"

"I can't remember anything."

"I don't understand you."

"Do you have to?"

"I want to, Celeste."

"Why?"

The iron mask of his face shuts, the reverberating clang almost audible in the room, and he answers, very, very carefully, "Just curiosity."

"Just curiosity?" you ask, probing.

"Just curiosity," he repeats with far too much emphasis.

"I don't think anything ever had a chance to be important to me," the words rush out, thrown off by the impelling motion of the vast wheel of memory slowly closing off in the dim cavern of your brain, and, helpless to stop them, you sit and watch. "When you're small, young, a child, nothing is really important. There are the small things you like, they seem important then, but they aren't things you can want as an adult. And by the time I was a teenager people always gave me what I wanted, before I could even ask for it. I always had everything I wanted. So there was nothing I could really come to want, because there was nothing I didn't have, and couldn't easily get. There wasn't anything to become important, I had it all, and nothing someone gives you can be important. I don't think it can. Something can't be important unless you have to work for it and struggle to get it and can't have it without a great deal of effort. I've never had to do that."

"Funny, it doesn't show, not in your face, not really in your voice," he pours cream into his coffee and without stirring it, sips it, "but isn't there anything you never had, anything at all you were never able to get, any question you couldn't answer?"

You shake your head, "No—" and stop, hard, the blazing shape of a question, that question, glimpsed, never formulated, never stated, never answered, searing across your mind. "Well . . . maybe one."

"What?" he asks, and the intensity of your answer is too great to stop, it comes hurtled out by the very bellows power of your lungs and the pumping action of your heart, as vital and necessary as the processes of your life: "Why do people want to sleep together, not fuck, but make love?"

"You're really serious about that, aren't you?" he asks, starting the engine and pulling out of the parking lot into the empty streets of the town, the low whir of his tires spinning over the pavement and a few clouds piling under the moon and covering the western stars.

You sag down in the seat, a thin smoke of exhaustion misting in your flesh, buckling the seat belt and letting the acceleration press you backward, trying to find an answer that will make him understand, but not finding it, finding only a never ending emptiness that contains no words at all. "Yes."

"I see."

There is a pause while he whips off the street and roars up the entrance ramp headed back onto the freeway, your ears filled with the full throated growl of an engine satiated by fuel, the night wind streaking by with the white flutter of moths trapped in the jet suction of the window, and the yawing direction of his questions blowing through your brain as you open your purse and take out another joint, lighting it from the dash and letting the smoke be sucked away by the air-conditioner. Then the heavy tilt of the car levels out into a dead straightaway and you race over the pavement, the red line of the speedometer climbing higher and higher while he glances over at you, then shifts his eyes to the rear-view mirror and looks back down at you, unable to start easily.

"You've been laid by a lot of men, haven't you?" he asks, hesitating over each word as if he knows that you are a person who cannot be offended by truth, this truth anyway, and that this is the truth, but has, from earliest childhood, been brought up in a world where men are not honest with women and don't talk to them about subjects like this, and does not, and never will, find it easy, this particular kind of honesty.

But his embarrassment is almost funny, if there were, ever, anything to laugh about, his blind determination that you are a woman who has been had many, many times, and in one way he is right, you have even, if you can imagine it, and burst through the surface of reality to the insane universe where it is true and see it in a double-screen image from both sides, had yourself, or had this body, which is now, anyway, yourself, and you have had, though he could never imagine how, countless orgasms, so there is a safe answer. "I guess you could say that . . . I've been laid a lot."

"I thought so," he says, more easily now that it's been agreed upon and brought out into the open, "I think I know what's happened. I don't think it's terribly unusual. At least, I think there are a lot of girls like you, or somewhat like you. You're different, though, and it isn't only your face, which looks so unused, it's . . . maybe just your honesty about every-thing, I can't say."

"You're not really very good at this, whatever it is you're trying to say," you reply, not meaning to be bitchy, but suddenly feeling that you just don't care anymore, the last dregs of the day emptying out of your soul and leaving you with a numbed depression that sinks through everything, and you wish his slow approach to his final point was shorter and less agonizing, because he is in agony, in pain, in some kind of doubt, and you are tired of filling people with pain and doubt, and maybe that is only because you are, for the first time, beginning to know fear and doubt and indecision and helplessness, and, as they always predicted you would, are now, through experience, experience you don't want, learning that the way you treated all those other girls was wrong, and that your own relentless disregard of people is something you may, someday soon, be sorry for. But another thin track of thought laces up through the first; how were you ever to know that all the other people you were playing with were any less automatic than yourself, how were you to know that the elaborate ritual they went through was anything more than a game they had invented but not explained to you, and if you had, surely you would have acted differently, but could · you have, could the cold ice citadel of your soul warm to anything unless it first felt warmth itself, and therefore knew that there was a warmth in others, because ice can know nothing beyond its own coldness and see nothing but coldness in others.

"No, damn it, I'm not," he answers, his fingers clenching into the yielding plastic of the steering wheel until the veins and tendons stand out on the back of his hands and his face is as immobile as carven jade, "but I'm trying, and you might have the decency to listen."

And his pain is, somehow, your pain and you wish you could reach out and touch him, the real him, and you are sure there is a real him, just as there is no real you, but know, having seen the question's shape, that there are real other people and that there should be a real you, even if you don't know what that would be like.

"I'm sorry," you say, reaching out and touching the back of his wrist, "I didn't mean it, and you didn't deserve it."

"Oh, fuck it," he says, jerking his hand away, his mouth twisted into a hurt, little-boy expression of rejection, "it's just that I think you've been had early and often by men, and they were all willing to pay something for it. Not a whore's payment, but . . . a mistress maybe, I don't know what the word in the middle is."

63

"Whore will do nicely," you hear your voice say, the words sliding smoothly out of the high.

"But," he shakes his head, ignoring you and plunging on, "but it doesn't matter what you call it, that's the kind of life you've had."

"I guess you could say that."

"Well, you've gotten used to it, too used to it, and you don't know any other way."

You put out your cigarette, which is a long way away at the end of the folded extension of your arm, grinding it against the lip of the ashtray. "That's right."

"And you can say it so evenly, so flatly so it has the ring of a terrible truth," he pushes a button and the car rides along at a steady hundred and thirty while he rests his feet on the floorboards.

"If you want the whole truth, and you know it, I went into that bar tonight looking for a man who's mistress I could become."

"I know that, I knew it when I first saw you in the mirror, knew exactly what you were after. But I have a different proposition to make you," he turns away from the road a moment, his eyes almost hidden in the night. "Only understand, there isn't any difference between it and any other you might get. Don't let that scare you. Just say the terms are a little different, that's all."

Here it comes, at last, the final destination, the ultimate goal of all the evening's twisted, tortuous paths, the meaning and purpose behind every masked and cautious question, his real, true motivation that he does not, even now, fully want to face, but hides, even from himself, during the last few seconds, glancing into the rear-view mirror and kicking the acceleration up higher as the car slides into the far left hand lane, but even while he does, you can sense, far back in the dimmer reaches of your mind, the looming form of his question and it lurches, abruptly, bearing unexpectedly down on you, huge and over-shadowing. But when he thumbs the speed back over to automatic, his face harder than any face you have ever seen, not even mask-like anymore, too empty and neutral to be anything, merely a wound of flesh, doughy and somehow repulsive, you know he has veered off into another tangent, narrowing the course of his approach; but unwilling, yet, to arrive, and he begins, "Look, you wanted to be kept by somebody, I understand that. For a very small, to you, I guess, service, a man gives you an apartment and money and leaves you alone most of the time."

He pauses and the silence presses by.

"And you've been had by many men, all of them willing to pay some kind of price to have you just because they were horny and you looked good and were willing to let them lay you. But I don't think you've ever been able to care about a guy, or been to bed with one you liked. You've probably never seen anything in guys to like. They were all just bodies interested in fucking you. I doubt if you've ever met a guy you liked, or felt desire. I think you're a screwed up girl who's never had a guy want anything from you but sex."

Again.

"Don't get me wrong, I'm no different than the rest. When I looked at you, I wanted you. I'm not some kind of holy reformer trying to get you to change your life. That's not what this is all about."

Again while you take out another joint and light it.

"But . . . well . . . it doesn't matter why, not to you anyway. I want something from you just like everyone else, and I'm willing to pay for it." There is the heart-beat hesitation of a wild change in subject, but coming closer, the glide path narrowing, "Do you know who I am?"

You shake your head through a smooth, hour-long arc, wondering how long he's been talking and how much longer he will take to finish, not impatient, your breath coming in so slowly and going out so slowly, but everything taking so damned long, and just curious how the quick track of time has become derailed through a country where every second hangs eternally before the fall of the next.

"I didn't think you did. Maybe I'm becoming too self-centered, or maybe it's just living with the people I do, but I produce environments. I don't create them, or direct them, or conceive them, I just put up the money and rake it in."

Again.

"And I rake it in. I have a great deal, more than enough, I think, to satisfy you."

And again.

"I want you to marry me."

The approach to Las Vegas looks strange at night, or dawn with the pale edges of false dawn fading from the sky into that blackest, darkest moment before the first edgings of the sun over the flat horizon into that instant desert daylight flashing, unobstructed, everywhere at once, blinding the night adjusted eyes, making even the players in their open-air casinos blink for the final rotation of a slot, or the final bounce of a ball, or the final flick of a card, but all this by day is only a multi-leveled soaring collection of spires erected on the war-blasted bones of the older city, all pale blue as the sun- streaked sky, and now, up ahead, hung in space, solid cubes of light burn, self-supported, a hand full of colored flares eternally frozen in the heavens.

But when the gray edge of morning spills over the ground and stains all the colors a dull muddish brown, the car pulls hungrily into the maw of a filling station, and you shake yourself out of a half-doze and look up at the pale plastic giants of the buildings coated with seasons of rain and dust baked together by the sun, unable to believe that any of this is happening and that in a few more minutes you will be . . . well . . . but more concerned, anyway, that you haven't been out of this dress and this underwear for almost a day and that you looked puffy-eyed and pale, wondering if, should he be serious, which you can't believe, he will go through it with a girl who looks like the one in the mirror before you, because this is some nitty-gritty moment that matters to your future and all you have now to carry you through it is your looks, and they had better be enough. The exhaustion of not-quite-enough sleep has eaten away your strength, and you don't even have the energy to look beyond the roots of the town and the bright flowers of the marquees, or lift your head when Howard says to the attendant, "Fill her up," and continues, pressing the button that rolls down the windows to let in a cool fresh breeze, "and can you tell me which way to city hall?" but are too awake to miss the attendants quick grin or Howard's responding glance over to where you appear to sleep against the door, a glance which must be questioning, because it is neither hard or masked, and the word you don't want to face bursts in your brain like stars, and the attendant's directions distract him before he sees the stiffening of your body.

You don't know why, exactly, you've agreed to this, there is no real why, maybe, just a moment's impulse, if you can believe that, or a realization that here, no matter how you handle it, is a security you never worried about, a future that will give you breathing room, thinking room to decide what you want to do, and give you money to do it with, because, you can, after all, get rid of Howard at the right time, and end up with a chunk of his money, and he will, no matter how anyone looks at it, have been using you for his own purposes, which he certainly is not bringing out into the open any more than you are. But if you were to look any farther than the turn of the next second, your mind would crack, split, smashed, cleaved open, totally spaced until the immersion left it as empty as the burned out remains of a bombed building, and you find another joint, lighting it and drawing the smoke down into the bottom of your lungs, watching the city begin to blur by again, rolling down your window, the breeze lashing you awake. An irresistible heaviness has lined the lids of your eyes, forcing them down, increment by increment, until only a thin crack of light seeps through and is gone, and the frame projection of life jumps like a broken film and the car is stopping in the middle of a cardboard-specked landscape that turns to stereoscopic reality with a slow revolving motion, and the three story glass cage of city hall is beside you.

None of this is real enough to believe, though the evidence of a bra that has somehow changed position as you slept and cuts sharply into one shoulder and breast and the clammy touch of the nylons on your legs is powerfully convincing, so you wait a moment while Howard locks the car, not wanting to start toward the imprisoning glass doors, leaded and gray with conspiracy, trapping the light and giving back only a silvered reflection of your own body small with distance, and he does, finally come up to you, and Christ, takes your arm, hesitating with light fingers and then holding it firmly at the wrist, guiding you forward. They have conveniently etched a sign into the doorway directing you upstairs for marriage contracts, and you both step into the elevator rising to the third floor and finding a wide, clean hallway, not quite lit by the early morning sun and take it, past banks of unopened offices to a gleaming room where two sleepy clerks are sipping coffee and eating breakfast, your stomach condensing into a dense knot moving with empty nausea on itself.

There are some brief forms to fill out and you can't think, mind-ripped, what name to use, until you remember that it doesn't matter, and sign Celeste Fuller, handing them back to the clerk who puts them on her desk, the pale pink of her blouse dark with wrinkles and sweat, and then takes your fingerprints, feeding them into their central computer and letting the electronic restructuring compare them instantly with every fingerprint in every central computer in every city in the inhabited states, and the realization that you don't know whether or not these hands and this body have ever been married, never bothered to ask, though you don't think so, but wonder, anyway, if there is some chance, you are still married, somewhere, to an utter stranger, and would that be any worse than marrying the utter stranger having his fingerprints checked with so many others to see if he is still married to someone, somewhere, standing beside you and frowning. But you aren't, either of you, and they slide a copy of the contract before you, requiring you to read every single word out loud and agree to every condition of community property division, and making him read it too, until they are sure you both agree and are willing to be bound to the standard form, and then witness your signing of it and, accepting their fee, turn you out.

"Want to eat first?" he asks casually, as you find yourself in the dazzling light of a Nevada morning, the question striking straight into the pain-axis of your stomach and leaving it harder than fused rock, and you know what comes second as surely as you know the shape of death and the greater shape of a question that never, now, seems to have been far from your thoughts, and you agree, reluctantly, though you remember having been hungry, but wanting, more than anything, to make time to meet your fate, not able to believe, now that it's here, that it is real or that you can face it, the loudness of your breath almost overwhelming.

In the diner, time begins to smear by again, words and sights and shapes melting into each other, and you find you have nothing more to say, that your answer and your signing were all you had in you, and he looks down at his steak and eggs as if not really believing them there, never taking his eyes off them, cutting into them and shoveling them into his mouth and chewing and swallowing but not seeming to notice, and your own, covert glances through lowered eyelashes, ease away whenever you think he might look at you, but he doesn't and you finish the meal in silence, not having spoken since you left the bureau, not wanting to, afraid that the weight of any communication might shatter your last walls of control and last images of yourself, dreading what has to happen to you now, and only hoping that you have gotten a high enough price for it. Then you are finished, both finished, and get up, throwing down a tip, and walk, not looking, not talking, not touching, out to the low dusty frame of the car, the wind, pressing your dress against your legs and blowing a few blades of grass down the streets, already hot and dry with the morning's sun fully over the horizon, and let yourself into the car, not daring, not wanting to speak even when he pulls into the parking lot of a motel and your eyes close, the oblong image of the sign still winking on and off behind your lids, listening, but not looking, as he says:

"Wait here, I'll register," perhaps sensing that having to sign, or see signed, that register the way it will have to be signed, would be more than you could take and that, if he is to get you into the room and his cock between your legs, because that's what it comes down to in the end, he will have to make it as easy as possible on you because you are, yes damn, you are, really on the edge of cracking and this man wants to fuck you, fuck you, fuck you . . . Insert here: one color Polaroid of a male, bent forward, hands on knees, cheeks of the ass spread, a giant phallus rushing toward it . . .

BLACKOUT.

4.

You don't remember the journey from the car to this suite, it doesn't seem to matter, the heavy drapes and the polarized windows cut down on the sun and it's almost dark enough to need the electric lights, but you don't want them, need, instead, the protection of the darkness and the sanctuary of not seeing, and close, once again, your eyes, as you have closed them so many times in the last few fragmentary moments, blanking out completely, for whole stoned moments, entire passages of time, filtering out the slices of reality too distasteful, too unreal, or just too damn human to take, and seeing everything in a frozen motioned blur too familiar to be frightening because, after all, nothing unusual is happening, nothing that hasn't happened a thousand million times before, nothing out of the ordinary, just a guy and a girl, he a little too restrained and nervous, even in the elevator, obviously wanting to touch you, but not daring for some reason, imagining, correctly, that a touch, even though for reasons he can't imagine, would freak you out, and wanting to be considerate, but wanting, also, you to know that it is only consideration that motivates him and not any kind of timidity, and, certainly not at his age, sexual insecurity, and he wants you to know it and to know that you know it, but also wants to be considerate, while you both realize that neither of you is exactly young or virginal or really has to take this any way but in stride, only, somehow, it is not being taken in stride by either of you, him because, maybe, if you are right, he sees something different about you which has made him, for whatever reasons, do this, and you, because this is not really anything that has ever happened to you before, are, for the first time in your life, scared screaming shitless and, needing somebody to comfort you, know, Hash, that it can't be him, even if he wants it to be, because he is here, also wanting to fuck you, and that is, now, sucked in with it all, and you trust him, or have to trust him, if that makes any difference, and

71

can't be held in the pure sexless comforting way you now need to be held, because, for him, and maybe for you, but especially for him, the sex is just too mixed in to prove anything, and he wouldn't be able to think of you as a person, but only as a sex object, or if not object, at least sex, and you only want to be held in a safe, comforting, you are sure, eternally sexlessly comforting embrace, with no other reason and purpose than that you are cared about as a person and not someone to be fucked, and then, if you could have that respite from all eternity and know that the war of life had declared a peace zone around you, you could do whatever it is you want, untouched by sex or anything. You could deal with all this, being a man and wanting, or do you want, women and being, for the reality of here and now, a woman and about to be taken to some kind of cosmic comic bridal bed and laid, and you want to go somewhere else, but there is, you know, nowhere else to go, and find yourself here, lying in bed, having stripped down to, but no further, underwear, which means, in the reality of breast and hip and body and vagina you don't want to admit, bra and panties, and are waiting with the covers pulled over you, needing, if only for a single second longer, to be hidden, waiting for him to come out of the bathroom and begin whatever has to begin now, thinking finally, shamefully, willing to crawl and admit crawling, if only there were some way out, that you have seen this scene from the other side too many times and that, perhaps, you deserve nothing else. So, finally, step by step, you have found yourself stripped down to this moment of sexual acceptance and reality that you could never have had, if, that first moment, so long ago, when you first grasped the shape of a question you have only tonight put into words, you had been a different person, and all the plastic empty moments of reality in your life, before and after, have only now come to have any meaning and only now do you see yourself, as what you were and what you are and see a conscious difference between the two, and this, you grasp, reaching behind and unhooking the bra, taking it off and leaving it under the sheets, is the first moment of insight you have ever had. He opens the bathroom door, sliding it to the

72

left and switching off the light, looking at you in the air-conditioned silence, dark and masculine, his body a male body you can't feel anything toward but a vague repulsion, never have, never will feel anything else but repulsion, for only women get you truly horny, but you do need, and he can't be the one to do it, to be held and loved, and have sex left out, and then, later, when you feel safe, brought back again, maybe, but is this any more than your own terror at what will be and is beginning to happen to you, or is it some ultimate spark, some human twinge, some reality of self you've never felt and never dared believe that you are now discovering when it is too late, realizing, finally, that you are after all a person even if the terror welling through your body is turning you a limp, docile plastic that he can have because you cannot, must not, dare not ever tell him or try to tell him because if this thing, this change you think is happening to you, this sudden discovery of the self is ever denied, or ignored, or not believed, nor cared about, it or you, or whatever you there is, will die, and never have lived beyond this terror filled moment of conception, and you want desperately to open your mouth and work your throat and say something he can hear and respond to and try to communicate with, but the terror is too heavy, crushing you beneath it, and the loud roaring of your breath overwhelms the room as he sits on the edge of the bed next to you, the mattress sinking under the weight and turning you slightly to him, and he puts his hand on your knee, pressing it through the covers. Then some strange chemical reaction of the stone, rushing into a whirlpool vortex of its own creation triggers a full sensory awareness, and your breathing grows louder and louder and louder, the silence heavier than before, and he pulls the cover down off one breast and suddenly your whole body is open to your inner sight, every psychological barrier crashing down, and you are there, a female, a person, in every pore and inch of skin because you have to be and are and must accept being that and its nature and use it if you are to survive, and isn't there, now, something more than just a need to survive, more than a basic animal drive to go on living no matter what the cost, a part of you that has learned, or is beginning to learn, to count the cost

73

and wants something more than just survival and hopes that there is something higher and better than what you have been and what you have had and more profound than all those animal couplings you went through with all those wet, willing girls before, in that other life, because you have seen it and sensed it and felt inside yourself a something, and been, tonight, conscious of it, as a reality, for the first time, but only in this situation, where you can't begin to explore it, but believe, and you never did believe before, that you can be a decent person, a person at all, and that sex, any kind of sex, could be groovy for you and a something you could share with someone and know it was a going from one of you to the other, a consciously controlled communication of your reality and theirs, and now, aware of your orifice and that imminence of being laid and getting fucked you know that you have finally made it to being a person, if self-awareness, fear and caring, wanting to be cared for, comforted and protected are being human; and you know that they are.

But the tissue-thin wafer of that second long eternity of insight is gone, and his face stubbled in the shadowy room, is moving toward your nipple and his lips are starting to part so you can see, behind them, the glistening tip of a tongue, his lids slide over the direct reality of his eyes, shutting whatever he is thinking in behind the impersonal skin-mask of his face, and you are left alone with a man who wants you for reasons you can't understand, and who is going to take you now, as his marriage right, and your own eyes seal off the last glimpse of the outer reality, room, face, bed and yourself, and surrender to the surface of your skin, seeking through it a deeper perception.

His tongue touches your nipple, his mouth hot and moist, saliva wet, the tip of the tongue a tiny, almost abrasive point moving slowly and relentlessly up and down along the side of the breast and back up, trying to stir the wrinkled flesh to life, failing, not knowing the failure is yours, not his, and sliding his hand down across you under the covers. You wish you could do something to help, something to · make him feel better, but your eyes are seared shut and the dry rasp of breath in your throat is a hollow silence you can't overcome while his hands move over your body, pressing down and in on the skin, caressing belly and hip, brushing past the coarse patch at the crotch, cupping thigh and knee, then returning, lightly, barely touching, to cradle your breast, squeezing gently, the ball of his thumb kneading the puckered teat. And the inevitable pneumatic pressure of his lips on yours happens, the unshaven barbs of his whiskers grating on your mouth, and you open it slowly, fully, passive, letting him have it, his tongue frantic and desperate, teasing the edges of your lips in long full strokes, trying to ignite some answering response, but you, plastic, wait, listening for each moment to pass, which he does not know and cannot guess and he works his way down your neck, his tongue restless, sucking the flesh of your shoulder into his mouth, raking it with his teeth as he pulls himself halfway on to you, the weight crushing down between your breasts and across your leg, fingers still playing on the flaccid surface of your nipple, the free hand tracing the shape of your ribs, and you wonder if this is, finally, what fucking is all about, though you can sense the growing touch of his shaft inching across your stomach, growing harder and bigger and rounder, and he eases over to the other side, one hand pressing down toward your crotch.

His finger parts the bristling hair and hangs for a moment, perched on the bluff of your vagina where the skin begins a final, irrevocable descent to the center of your being, then it slips over the edge, questing among the dry folds of flesh for your clitoris, smoothing out each convolution between thumb and forefinger until it reaches its destination. Like the pressing of an electrical switch your body arcs, the current running in a coaxial line between the muscle sheathing of your guts and the inner surface of your flesh, a need that stretches from pubis to throat, erupting in your mouth, tongue moving restlessly over your own lips, heavy with the salt taste of sweat, but the bowel-clenched fear of womanhood blocks it off, sealing it beyond your reach, and the flesh driven needs of your body have an existence far from the citadel of your mind where the stoned receptivity of your brain senses everything, experiences nothing. His left hand massages the back of your neck, while the right thumbs the stiffened ridge of your clitoris and his mouth circles in a narrowing vulture's swoop the unaroused valley of your nipple, his breath short and heavy, louder, even, than your own.

His finger slips down through the moist tissue of your cunt, drawn by desires older than time, following, in its thick, stubby immensity, the plunge of your womb, entering the walls of your vagina, forcing them apart, filling them with just a finger, filling your whole body from crotch to throat, crushing in the passages of your digestive tract, squeezing your lungs back against the unyielding marrow of your spine, and you reach down along your body, fumbling for the erect hardness of his prick, afraid to discover its size, knowing how big it must be and that the slow fingerfucking motion of his hand is already more than you can stand, opening your mouth to scream, but closing, instead, your fingers around the palm-breadth of his phallus, wondering how it can be so much bigger than yours was, for yours took this body easily and his will surely rip you asunder. But there is no time even to protest, and you can only be thankful that your period had stopped by the time you left the restaurant and you were able to remove the tampon, because his hand is withdrawing, sliding inevitably to the knee and his determined tongue is, even now, lapping at your navel, probing into the defenseless center of your stomach, inching steadily down into the brushcountry of your pubic hair; and now the long hungry extrusion is reaching, will reach, has reached the unavoidable point of all arousal and flicks, with a caress so light it is almost non-existent, across that one betraying moist fragment of flesh, and the milk-gray color of need bursts against the gut-tight fear stretched across your loins, leaving the ego workings of your brain cold and remote from the hollow need to be filled building in your cunt.

But the spaced-out, semi-circular rimming protrusion of his tongue into the echoing caverns of your body, sliding with a ricochet reverberation from surface to surface through a matrix of intersecting angles that is, after all, almost, but not quite, reaching the very center, midpoint, implosion core of your sexuality, withdraws, the speed, radius, width decreasing, slowing down and coming out, spiraling from the unreached nova molten chalice of your womb, to the inflamed gaping lips and out, down the leg, leaving a wet slime trail, to the crooked dimple of the knee; and he works his way back up, his head re-orienting, shifting, his weight easing on to your sweat slickened flesh, and you almost wish that his tongue had been a prick, or that, somehow, he had reached that nestling, untouched spot where the sex explosion of your cunt and the head eruption of his prick merge in that ultimate communication between people that you sense can now take place, has, a million times before, taken place, and is the final goal and drive of being human, but instead, because the surface powered fear, that something you aren't in control of may happen and agonizingly destroy, paranoid though the thought may be, the real you surfacing through the twisted empty warps of mind and soul and body, you have lain here, unresponsive, and he has felt it and is dragging himself up to talk to you, and now you can sense being both him and yourself, so, whatever happens afterwards, you, right this instant, love him and are alive, and want him, when everything else is settled, to make love to you, and he, raises his head, looking down into your eyes, and says, "What's wrong?" and, not being able, yet, to explain any of it, you lie.

"Nothing. Go on," wanting him to be happy and willing to fake your reaction, making him think that the sights and sounds you respond with are the ones he must have and, after all, has a right to expect, not knowing that you aren't at all what you seem, and that the stark, tight barrier damming every uncoiling watt of excitement is a fear he can't understand and you won't explain, wish you could explain, but are driven through an endless falling terror too great to resist, and can find nothing to cling to to slow the awful plummeting acceleration building in chest and groin, not even his body with your arms locked around it, crushing your chest to it, trying, with legs hooked behind his, to press into the sanctuary-dead calm behind the muscle, skin and bone shield he makes in the wind-blown, ocean-deep storm breaking about you. So you find, in the undertow rushing from your brain through your body and finally hurtling into those unknown reaches beyond the ego awareness of your own flesh, that you, for reasons you cannot quite put into words but can feel and see on the paisley overlay pattern of his face, want him to feel like a man, like a human being, not hurt him because of your own stupid twisted reactions, not, unnecessarily, make him feel like a failure when the girl he thinks you are, and you have led him to believe in, fails to react the way she should if he is doing his job, and for no other reason anyone could ever imagine.

His eyes have the slightly tightened, eyebrow-knitted, narrowness of a man puzzled, wanting an answer and willing to be soothed, the second before hurt look that cries out for comfort, mutely, but visibly, not daring to ask, willing to bear the pain of solitude before the greater agony of rejection; and you smile, knowing it only too well, worrying and caring least he too should have to bear it, sliding your hands up into his tangled hair, palms on his cheeks, and pull his face down, closing your eyes and pressing your lips against his, hearing, distantly, the dual conflict of need and terror, but protected by the enveloping warmth of making another human happy. Your mouths meet and you let his be the victor, yielding to his tongue, making yours answer back, though what you actually want to do is turn over and curl up in the strain-free fetal comfort of sleep, losing the necessity of now in the serenity of escape, but your teeth rake gently against his tongue and you draw the air from your mouth into your lungs, sucking him into the vacuum chamber of your throat, caressing the animal wet finish of his palate, fingers passing his rib cage, one hand cupping his hip and the other reaching between the grinding hollows of the pelvic girdles to grasp the swollen shaft of his penis and guide it to the indented tunnel of your womb.

The whirlpool lurchings of reality converge in the receptive flesh of your vagina, the mass motion of life fragmenting in the choked stream, sight and sound, past and present grinding themselves into infinitely small discreet units, each rebounding with lightning-blast speed through the bone

78

prison of your skull, flashing past sight and consciousness and then disappearing forever through the apex funnel of your uterus, drawn or driven through a metaphysical passage and emerging, somehow, into a greater awareness of the universe outside, and it is all nothing more than the word-symbols clung to by your mind as the corona of his prick invades, pressing forward and then pulling backward, and pressing forward again, but always farther in than the last time, the unbreached chalice of your body. He is, everywhere, inside you, and you seem to hold his immensity as much inside the stretched fabric of your skin, legs, arms, mouth, chest, face, brain, transfixing even ultimately, your soul, whatever that is, a slender shaft, for all its size, driven through your ego, as inside the single vessel of your cunt. You take, as he comes as far in as it seems he can reach, the unyielding bone of his pelvis rammed immovably against yours, filling everything now so there is no you left in the body, but only the necessary solidity of him, a deep breath, clenching your fingers into his flesh and jerking your mouth away from his, resting your chin on his shoulder, looking over his back at the flowing plastic unreality of the ceiling, so that he cannot see the fact of the game you are playing for him in your face, breathing artificially and hoarsely into his ear, driving any thought but the molten need in his loins from his mind.

Your throat moans, the air forced past the constriction of mouth and tongue, not entirely pretense, the sound a melding of fear and tension and necessity as your back arches against him and, listening to the rhythm of his breath, your lungs make shallow, excited sounds, the speed of his phallus race-horse swift, driven by a human desperation and aching you, of all the women in the world, understand only too well. Then his fingers slip under your arms and clench in your shoulders, the nails cutting sharply into the flesh, his breath begins to suck in, in, in, the hissing sound of the inhalation going on and on as if this were the last he may ever take and he has to make it as long as possible, and he thrusts against you with a motion so powerful it should be the tearing, rending agony of a lifetime, but is, somehow, muted into a wonder so penetrating it must

79

be flooding from every pore, and the heat of his sperm explodes within the banked oven of your womb, blazing through every neural pathway of your brain, searing him and his memory forever into your flesh.

The face of the earth is changed beyond recognition and the cross-connected web of your senses is a jumbled chaos, unable to resolve anything it contacts, the cry of your breath in the wonder of his climax a stark indigo, your own desperate need of a future fulfillment like the c-flat string of violins, and the pressure of his weight a sense of overpowering height, and the sounds of your vibrating body, unsatisfied, but capable of satisfaction, are to him, the sounds of a woman he has conquered; but the terror, the blinding, overwhelming terror that is a red wave through the universe, is the terror of an animal trapped, broken, and owned, and the frantic word ESCAPE is a command you cannot avoid.

PART THREE
Retribution

1.

In the crazed evening sunlight Las Vegas has the gray pallor of exhaustion, the dull insanity-tinged hue of a city sick and rotted with despair, the chunky, still pale, neon signs of the casinos and bordellos are like something vomited out by a world crushed in the post-atomic depression of a third great war, a war that looks like "the war to end all wars," after all, because no one has the energy left to fight another and because the love-hip, mind-blown youngsters in the new governments will never let another be started; but in the half-second's disorientation as you emerge, staggering, into the crowded streets, barely comprehending the frantic madness of holiday jubilation, it is merely the uttermost hell of some cosmic bummered drug trip whirling away from all true reality, and, though you cannot quite grasp why you have fled, panicked, from the room above, mind as desolate as any bomb-blasted no-man's land, this is still better than the womanmarried tightness of that room, and, maybe here, you can recapture the true, valid, real reality of being Andre Fuller, repeating your name over and over endlessly, trying to find some relation between it and the soft-reflected-dark-haired girl you see in every window and the sexual hunger you see in every male. But the moment's illusion wavers and the city solidifies, leaving only a transparent hope that it is not real, that nothing is real, the surfacing desire to turn back, by brute force, the hands on the clock of time and undo all the world's changes, and that, too, vanishes, drawn into some thoughtchain's undertow, and you see, looking out of your eyes, a town founded on the need of a nation weary unto death, see its buildings and people and climate as you have never seen anything, anyplace before, as if the optic nerve, all your nerves, had, all your life, been clogged with the mucus of futility, and now, sucked clean by a fear greater than any emotion should be, it, and they, are finally, fully alive.

You do not know just where it is you are going, only that you are fleeing the shattering instant of acceptance, when you bent before the gray metal reality of what you are and became, for a heartbeat, a woman, and you must get as far from his room and his bed and his marriage and his face as possible, because it is not as easy as you thought, and, brick by brick, the stoned wall of indifference you so carefully erected, joint by joint, through all those endless hours, is crumbling, and the hard cold truth of intercourse is more than you can now, or ever could, take, and anything, work or death or anything, is preferable to being a woman, and you want, right now, to have a woman, any woman, and experience that desire in whatever ersatz form. And comes, unsummoned, the memory image of him lying, asleep, on the rumpled, stained clothing of the bed, his penis shrunken and dark as you stood by the dresser, a faint, stomach-cramping moisture running down the inside of your thigh, and you stop, outside the hotel, laughing, one hand spread on the cool plastic wall, looking through and at the crowd, not quite sure what to do next.

Your eyes hurt, aching with the constant pressure of light on retina, and the transparent irrelevancy of the city to what you want is almost visible, the scrambled nerve trunks of your perceptions still refusing to make sense out of the surroundings, and you know that none of this, men and women, lights and sound, can help you in any way, that there is a deeper, basic human core that must, instantly, be satisfied, healed, soothed, lotioned and balmed. The striding pace of the outer pedwalks moves off toward the distant edge of the city, traveling to buildings you can't make out, buildings at least different from the ones here, buildings that might offer some help to your needs, and you cross among the intent slabs of people circling in orbits far removed from your own path, the Hat crack of each step jarring up through heelbone and ankle, knocking a little of each breath from your chest and turning the world darker for lack of air, your dress, pulled on forever ago, yesterday morning sticky, and clinging to your unwashed skin, and, not able to halt a continual flow of wishes, you wish you, in a male body, or even, since there is no other choice, in this one, could stand under the needle spray of a shower until every trace of horror is washed away.

The pedwalk unrolls through the pasteboard facades of the casinos, past names so cute and contrived you are sure no sane mind conceived them and the owners are demented creatures who have never once experienced the reality of being human, and, thinking back, you wonder if anyone has experienced it as deeply as you, fitting the bits and pieces of your own life back into a bailing wire and chewing-gum personality that is certainly not your own, but the only one you are capable of, and you are too godawful weary to search for another.

These people, what can they imagine they are doing, can they be as game-playing and escape-seeking as they look, don't they have any grasp of the nature and importance of reality, or are they as unconcerned as they seem, don't they know life and death and tears and excrement as you do, or have they, in some alchemist's way, slid by all that into days as empty as this? Their faces are all as blank and dead as alabaster, as fixed and unseeing as carven stone, more bewildered than a child's, less than a child's, when did you ever see a child as removed from the world as they, as carefully wrapped in cellophane as they; were you, or any of them, that way as children, and if you weren't, why are you today; have sex and life and love no meaning, no relation to this mass of bodies worn by . . . what, you are not sure. There are so many different bodies and clothes and people, a multitude sculptured by some visionary from one mammoth block of porphyry, no single figure distinct and separate, only a topography of indentations and spaces suggesting hundreds but remaining, always, a mere homogeneous mass.

You try, for the life of you, knowing that you have to, have to, make some sense out of the multiverse around you, to find some relationship, some relevance, some common ground between you and the people milling by as the pedwalk carries you slowly along the criss-cross patterns of their lives, past the whirlpool emptiness of their celebration, that, remote from anything you know to be important, leaves you so untouched. But the blank, roaring static of the crowd is as dry and useless as the sandfiltered desert wind sucking the moisture from your veins, scouring face and flesh clean, a gritty clean, hot and uncomfortable, and, if you could find either the desire to move or the energy, you would flee through the mazed automatons masquerading as humans, and seek the cooler sanctuary of slot machine–banked lobbies, but your legs do not move and you travel helplessly by the pinwheel marquees of the casinos.

The sharp edge of the town draws nearer, it does not die away slowly in the fashion of less sophisticated cities, gasoline station by motel by used car lot, but ends, abruptly, with the scalpel-cut of a towering hotel, and beyond it lies only the colorless drab of the desert and a silver geodesic dome mushrooming on the empty plain. The buildings, after all, are only hollow constructions of plastic and metal, having nothing to do with the realities of life and death, nothing to do with the question that has driven you since that stoned, drugged plunge, arms out, feet together, helplessly falling, into the core of reality, and, now, question and answer are fused, and you wish, though none of this could have come to pass otherwise, that it had all never happened, the killing and the change, and that you could be Andre Fuller, but you are Andre Fuller, once more, but now you would be a different Andre Fuller, are a different Andre Fuller, one who knows what it is to be alive, and that others are alive, an Andre Fuller who knows and cares for, dearly cares for, all those darling wonderful girls you fucked all those other perfectly meaningless times, only it has taken all this, death and change and, you guess, re-birth, to make you aware of humanity, everyone else's and your own, of your life, of your breathing, even now, terrified and faint, life, and of the deep crying, flesh and gut and bowel-deep crying, need to be cared for and protected that can, ultimately, only be expressed in the flesh and gut and bowel-deep essence and embrace of intercourse, and, now that you cannot have them, you wish you could have them again, only a few, to love as they deserve to be loved; and it is the people in and around the buildings, who should, but don't seem to, be concerned by life and death, by the wonder of their own flesh and its necessities, by the bowel deep things that did not concern you, until the landscape of the universe altered. They are not anyone you can, this moment, and possibly any moment in the future; but you hope that's wrong, because it would be a lonely future, be concerned by or reached by or, really, yourself, care about, and you do need to be cared about and to care, and you are are are Andre Fuller, and the man in that room back there, Mr. Howard Sladek, may be legally married to this body, the husband of this female body which you have chosen to call Celeste, but can never be the husband of the shaking flesh bowel gut deep core that you have to believe is you, Andre Fuller.

A step ahead the pedwalk dies away to roll back upon itself and begin a mile behind, and, unthinking, automatically, from the habit of half-a-lifetime, you go forward, onto the asphalt flaggings, staring ahead at the weed-choked desolation, the wind stirring through the grasses, and then look up, at the front of the geodesic dome, its sectored walls reddish with the brimstone of sunset, its weathered silver surface older, perhaps, than you, framed by two poles, each bearing a sign, the left a crux ansata, the right a skull over crossed bones, and painted above the entrance: LIFE AND DEATH — the convergent truth of the universe, and from inside is a light blacker than extinction.

Inside is a light blacker than extinction, inside is extinction, inside is no reality at all . . . there is only and just barely, an encapsulated moment when you are in the threshold, the opaque impregnated air-curtain blowing simultaneously up and down your body, from right to left and from left to right, all at once, blacker than extinction on the outside, dead pitch black with the blackness of light sucked into an infinity of emptiness, mirror silvered without even the faintest hint of silver in the depths, or any depths, on the inside, perfectly reflective and non-existent, and in between, in that encapsulated moment, there is only the sense of being somewhere, of being, and nowhere, and then you are through and nowhere at all.

"Earthfire!"

86

The music is not music, it is sound, and it is not sound because it cannot be heard, it is something more than solid, it is metaphysical, it is not loud, loud is painful, it is more than loud, greater than loud, it has a volume that surpasses sound, you cannot hear it, though you can, almost, see it, and you know it is there, the marrow of your bones vibrates with it, the floor vibrates with it, the quivering, formless, unreal shapes of the universe vibrate with it, it is the ultimate rhythm, the music of the spheres, the single filling primeval sound, the sound of all beginnings and all ends, the tempo of sex, the beat of your heart, the rhythm of the universe, it engulfs the room and the lightstruck worshippers swirl through it.

"*Moonfire!*"

There is no reality, they have struck the set of reality and carted it away to the storage place of lost worlds, they have folded earth and sky, men and women, stars and hell into bright checkered squares and packed them deep in a cedar chest until, `someday, the acrid taste of nostalgia calls them forth once more, they have flung you, shocked, into the limbo of unclean souls to be blown through perdition until the end of eternity; there is no floor, there is no ceiling, there are no walls that stretch in a three hundred and sixty degree closed curve from behind you to behind you again, there is only darkness, no, not darkness, there is light, it is a void, a limbo, the ultimate environment.

"*Starlight!*"

A sweet-sour smell clings to your nostrils, the exact lingering ripeness of lemon pie, the freshly baked tang of yellow filling and brownwhite meringue, it is frighteningly familiar, as familiar as the odor of bitter almonds remembered from the California-matchwood cluttered interior of her apartment, and you take a breath, a good long breath, savoring, tasting, trying to recall, and hold it, paralyzed, unable to move a muscle, the semi-voluntary action of your lungs stopped, held still by an effort that is not will but pure drenching terror, recognizing the scent that is not, exactly, MST, but is still, for you, deadly enough, a crystalline alkaloid vaporized and re — circulated through the hidden orifices of the air-conditioners until each breath is a slightly higher stone culminating in a transcendental awareness that passes any understanding.

"The center of all things!"

You take a step back, the breath still in your lungs, afraid to exhale and draw more into your body, afraid to hold any longer, as, each moment, the blood pumping through the moist tissues of your lungs, is draining more and more of the chemical into your wine-red, slick salty stream of life, and you pivot, starting for the door, but there is no door, there is no wall, there is no room, there is neither depth nor breath or space, there is only you, the flesh sheathed container of your body alone in a kaleidoscopic unreality where the patterns and shapes of light shift faster than the speed of thought, and you can see nothing, as you can hear nothing, only reach out blindly, seeking . . . anything; the pulsing lightshow collage of images comes from somewhere behind the perfect reflectivity of the walls, spilling across darkness against people where it clings leech-like to their indistinguishable bodies, and against the mirrored surface of the walls, reflecting back into the opposite mirror, and then back, and then forward, and back and forward, endlessly, drenching the room, covering it, filling it with the rip-tide of insanity, drowning, suffocating you in the liquid thick immersion, and your hand touches, unexpectedly, the warm, bare satin of naked flesh.

"Be animal. Be man!"

A bright web of pain eats into your lungs and, explosively, they start up again, expelling the stale air and dragging in fresh, drug-laden madness, the sharp edge of the scent dulled by exposure, and you cough, staggering forward, fingers sliding over a hard masculine chest, an unseen hand, big and tough, closes over yours, yanking, catching you off balance and dragging you closer.

Now you know, remember, the broken machinery of your brain beginning to function again in the super-lubricated moment before STONE, the inescapable reality of your environment a trap you couldn't have, could you, expected, a one way ticket, here and now, to salvation, a purging of all earthly sins, a straight funnel into the new religion, and the man's hands, or the half-sensed pressures you think are the tips of his fingers and the shape of his palm, come down on you, one at shoulder, one at waist, and hesitate a moment, almost recoiling at the unexpected contact with clothing, and then, deftly, begin to unfasten them.

Another body brushed past you, and, though you can't see or hear them, you know, by some mystic means, that the temple is packed with bodies fused in the stoned, high, profound act of fucking, and that, in a moment, when the buzzing force already starting to pound into your brain fills it, you will, inevitably, join them; and you fight, with the last flickerings of clarity, to break free:

and, unexpectedly, you are, torn loose by the force of a strange arm on yours, ripping you free, the thin material of your dress, still held by your attacker, and he is your attacker, and he is the attacked, having come expecting, as he has every right to expect, the stoned monumental fuck of the drug and expecting everyone else to expect it too, ripping, the cloth opening to your belt, a current of air chilling the sweaty skin along the tops of your breasts, and you take another breath, not caring anymore, if it is drugged, and your head is jerked back, your mouth, opening in protest, filled with the desperate urgency of a male tongue.

"*Copulate!*"

This is it, this is Dionysus, the high mass of the new order, the great renewal ground where they impregnate the air with aphrodisiacs, hallucinogens, and contraceptives, where mankind comes to cleanse his soul in the furnaces of flesh, and you try to twist away, your hands searching through empty air for the solidity of the wall, head moving with the whip of your body, and the white-second Hare of a strobe pinlights the room and the coupling humans in it, sculpting the man above you from gray stone, a tall, lanky young man with a deep tan and hair bleached by sun or bottle, his face milkshake pale in the after image of the light, and you are pulled free by another set of arms, and, legs caught by a sprawled body, roll to the floor.

A wave of pearls engulfs you, iridescent showers of lotus petals raining with sandalwood softness across your flesh, gleaming droplets of rain burning with the gentle chill of a snowflake; you are drenched in a rainbow sea of tears, lost in the endless void of the universe, tumbling through the vast and starry heavens, bathed in the fiery splendor of worlds gone mad, surrounded by the intermingled plasma of a thousand million suns, embraced by a nova's warmth, sinking into the implosion core of the cosmos. Your brain contracts, broken loose from the moorings of your skull, shrinking instantly to microscopic size and hurtled, on an undertow current of indigo, through the sub-ethnic cavern of your body, watching the red-black pulsings of your blood through the intermeshed, interwoven, interconnected webway of veins, blinded an inexhaustible number of times by the blue-white spark of consciousness flashing five billion times a second through the synaptic ends of nerves, the layer upon layer, that you can see through a multi-ordinal vision from an infinity of viewpoints simultaneously, of redmeat muscle, sliding in a blood lubricated smoothness, across itself, revolving past the crater-pored paleness of breathing flesh, the black workings of kidney, heart and liver, the flaming factory of the lungs, to the hollow vessel of the womb and the receptive passage of the vagina.

The bright yellow impacted pain between floor and mind filters the strobe and you see again the tall, lanky young man with the dark tan and bleached hair leaning toward you, face triple imaged as if you had seen it before . . . before now, in some other life, and should remember it, but the thought quick faces of the Beatles shutters into your eyes, crisscrossed with the trinity grouping of Baez, Dylan, and Leary, and your head spins, gyroscopically unstable, your body following, twisting along the grid axis of the spine, and you roll to him, caught in the magnetic mind flux of the stone.

Twin ribbons, menthol-iced pastel, spiral endlessly through each other, a sinuous latticework erupting from your head and vanishing in the corkscrew fibers of your cunt, sucking the whirlwind blackness of the universe through your body, shattering the sky with the thunderous bellow of its echoes; earthquake thicknesses of music like slabs of freshly

90

baked bread fall in metrical order, piling higher and higher until the unremitting dandelion pressure of the notes crowds against you, coating skin and bone with an oil-slick cotton dampness, pounding with the true grit smoggy irritation of flesh on flesh, his fingers hooking behind your arms and pulling you together on the heavy parched wasteland floor.

The frozen motor of your mind, stopped in its endless whirlings by that panicked first second's immersion in the church, by the sheer, overwhelming finality of the trap into which you have led yourself, gives one last lurch, a terminal thought in the chain of thoughts linking the beginning of your life with now, a moment's rebellion against the brobdingnagian high lifting you and stoning you from all contact with reality, and you wish, as you seem to have spent your life wishing, that it were already over, what is beginning to happen, knowing that it will, eventually, be over, but wanting it over, so you can go on living, now, even as you surrender yourself to it, having no choice, sliding your tongue against the wet flower roughness of his, the chemical need, which has entered your blood and become physical, the artificial desire which is now real, consuming you, soul and body.

You hold him, palms and arms caressing his back, alive to his Hash, making of his Hash a banquet, touching, with the trembling vision organ of your hands, his body, his Hash, his being, wanting to know, beyond all knowing, his body, his awareness, his sexuality, whoever he may be, wanting beyond all wanting, something inside that vast hollowness between your legs, stuffing it, filling it, satisfying it, using it, enjoying it, your own body, reeling from the night's mind alone to the day on fire, bound by an electric sheath, welded by an alternating current, now from him into you, now from you into him, inescapably to his body. Your tongue is mad, shoulders and hips and calves crushed against the soft mirror-surfaced floor, for the taste of him, licking heavily over his lower lip, sucking it into your mouth and teasing it gently with your teeth, his own tickling the channel of flesh just below your nose, and you bend forward as his hands find the snap of your bra, unhooking it, and fall back as it peels away, your breasts sagging free.

But he is still unseen, a stranger your memory tries to trick you into believing you've known from somewhere, and the afterimage of his face is lost in the butterfly incandescence blazing in your eye, and your body betrays you, your mind betrays you, following the needs of flesh down long winding roots to the center of that need, telling you, truthfully, and that is the awful insidious part of it, that it is the truth, and you know it, and that it is only how you look at the truth that makes a difference, telling you, the while, overlaying and underlaying all thought, that he, whoever he is, is a human being with all the human blood and bowel needs, and hungering as desperately to be cared for and held as you are, were, must, and that here is as good a place as any to express them. And it is the truth, the terrifying truth, that you are both here, holding each other, both human, both flesh and bone, both alone in a universe of immeasurable loneliness, both burning with a cell-deep need for union, for the completion of the split-identified creature that is man-woman, both alive and breathing, and chemically, artificially, but still physically aroused, and both wanting it right now, here, on this mirror-tiled floor, engulfed in lights and sounds and writhing bodies, unable to see, unable to hear, unable, at last, even to feel, able only to sense, to be aware, to be conscious and to be conscious of consciousness, able only to be alive.

His mouth is fire, it is liquid fire, it is sight and sound and feeling and consciousness, all together, it is the direct perception of his being, it is fire poured from your mouth down your throat, it is a pleasure as keen as pain, it is a sensation so pure your breath stops in your lungs and your blood freezes in your veins and the walls of your vagina expand in the anticipation of his entry, and you want your flesh, your body, your cunt, stuffed and filled with the engorged shaft of his prick, with the swift sure charge of his loins, and his legs outside yours, and his prick, hard, hot and swollen against your belly, pressed between your stomachs, and his chest, painfully heavy against the sagging weight of your breasts, all seek to enfold you, but, instead, you are delivered up into him, are looking down at the chromatic void of your flesh, know his need, the pressure at the base of his tumescent tool, and want, want with a wanting beyond all imagining, to have him, whoever he is, buried within the oven of your womb, and would almost want, if some tiny pinprick of fear did not still remain in the farthest reaches of your mind, and if you did not know that the iridescent air is as laden with contraceptives as with madness, to feel and see, as you can now, stoned, see, the flowering of his seed in your body, but that is madness, and you are mad, and you, Andre Fuller, reel before the onslaught of womanhood, and feel the firm anchor of your body tear free from the whimpering grasp of your ego.

His tongue on your nipple and the rim of his opened mouth on your breast are a moist cavern of ecstasy and you arch your back, trying to push through the textured surface of this dimension into some other, where you can vanish down his throat, vanish into his flesh, merge with his body, reach the ultimate destination of release from this pleasure too sharp to bear, because it's all over now, everywhere, in every cell, in every fiber, a vast network of need and pleasure and love, a stronger and stronger insanity and greed and excitement blossoming with flame and fire and creation where flesh touches flesh, even your own touching your own, and all flesh is one, and you slide your hands down his ribs, prying the sweat-joined bodies apart, and wrap your fingers around the hot shaft of his prick, wanting it, if that is the way, to bring you release and salvation.

The fused growlings of your bodies pinwheel around the starpoint of your consciousness, ripped loose from you, and your need screams and screams and screams to be answered, not to fuck, or to be fucked, but to be answered, and by any means, and you want, not some beautiful girl lying with the dark triangle of her cunt open before you, but this man, right here, on top of you, and his prick in your hand, but want it, instead, in your cunt, and want him to drive and drive until you and he, both, collapse in the blessed, wonderful aftermath of climax. And his mouth releases your nipple, working lower while he backs off and hooks his fingers in the material of your dress and pulls it away, panties and dress, past knees and ankles and feet, leaving your crotch open, your legs free, and his tongue crosses the roughness of the pubis, and, as his arms go under your legs, lifting them, enters the crying flesh of your cunt. His mouth slides past, barely tasting, the agonized clitoris, and his tongue sets ablaze the very corridors of your womb, following the vagina in an impossible distance, draining its juices, giving you the first tastings of what the immensely bigger protrusion of his prick will be like, and you want him to hurry, to raise the fire into a conflagration and then take you, take you and satisfy that towering, aching hunger.

And he does, his mouth comes back and clamps on yours, fastened by your mutual insanity, and his prick, that hot, welcome prick, comes, ever so slowly, into you, on and on and on, driving you out, filling the latticework citadel between mind and cunt, blasting you from your body, so there is no you, only body, splitting Andre Fuller, prick, stud, and whore, he of the smiling, eternally smiling face and empty onyx eyes, forever from the quivering ecstasy of your ego, filling all needs, pulling out and coming in, out and in, out and in, out and in . . . building both of you, carrying both of you, sending both of you into a higher and higher realm where the crying agonized need becomes something greater than need, greater than either of you, and your cunt clasps his prick in a death struggle, tighter and tighter, the pressure so vast your body breaks under it, and as he slams one final, desperate time into you, the pressure blows, your cunt unleashes, and you hurtle out past the infinite bucking releases of his come, barely feeling the burning eruption of his sperm in your womb . . .

PART FOUR
Expiation

1.

From the moment the driver had slowed to pick her up, standing outside Santa Fe in the day old paper shift, thumb out, looking tired, exhausted, and ratty, she had known he would try to make her, just as she had known the driver who took her from Vegas to Santa Fe would not, from the first moment she had seen him, but the other had known, as she climbed in the car and they headed for Joplin, through some male chemistry she no longer understood, that she would let him, though he could not know, and could not suspect, that she would let any male, any male who asked her, use her body, out of pity for him, and out of pity for herself, thinking, knowing that if Celeste Fuller could find pity for others, they might find pity for her, and knowing that she needed pity and caring and love, and was never likely to find any.

The car rattled through the isolated darkness of the Oklahoma farm lands, the earth as dry and dusty as the morning's aftertaste of an all night grass trip, and the unwinking night, empty of houses, towns, and lights, lay flat and black around them, broken only by the distant radiance of a farm. They seemed to have come, for all that she could tell, half the distance of a lifetime since she had gotten in, traversed the continent since noon, the unchanging barrenness of the landscape the surreal creation of some despondent artist so that every mile was like every other mile and each farmhouse like every other farmhouse. Inside the steady growl of the engine pressed up warm and thick around her as she sat, curled, the trembling violence of the window against her cheek, and, outside, the first chill pangs of winter cut through the autumn night, limning the fields with frost. Only the top of Black Mesa had been hot, the descent growing colder and colder until they emerged on the flat wintery plains, the sweep of the wind unobstructed from horizon to horizon, and she rolled the windows up, shivering in the thin fibers of the dress, not having realized, after the heat of Angeles and Vegas, that the world would be anything but stifling.

Now they shot down the deserted road, the faded line in the center running from a microscopic dot in front, to a microscopic dot in back, never gaining, never losing, always steadily in the center. She knew, by the glittering intentness of his eyes and the suddenly licked away smile at the edges of his mouth, that he wanted to fuck her, would have wanted to fuck any passably attractive girl, and that, though unbathed and tattered, she was still attractive, knew that he wanted to feel attractive himself, capable of attracting a girl, capable of fucking her and satisfying her and himself, capable of getting-what everyone wants to and does get, someway, sometime in their life, and she knew that she would let him fuck her, let him feel capable, no matter how incapable he might be, because he was a human and needed her, if only for this one time, and it was good to be needed, something she could not refuse, not now, not after everything, not anymore.

The dim rectangle of a mileage sign flashed past, the weed-grown after image hanging in her sight for minutes, and she sighed, stretching, shifting her head back on the seat and twisting it around, trying to wring out the exhaustion of sleepless days and wired nights. It had been, man, days, since the morning before the wedding she did not, even now, want to think about, since she'd slept more than a few brief hours snatched in the seat of a car, and a dozen minutes, spaced out, on the floor of the dome. She needed, more than anything else she could imagine, to go to bed, to go to sleep, and eventually, to go to New York, or what had become New York, on the southern banks of the Housatonic across the Sound from the ruins of the original city. She needed to go there, or anywhere as far from Los Angeles and Howard Sladek as she could get, and in the dim, reconstruction turmoil of the East, she could lose herself in an anonymity of confusion.

"Wow," he whispered, laying his smoldering joint in the ashtray, and she reached out, picking it up between thumb and forefinger, the mentholated tip springy as plastic, taking a deep hit, "this is only Alva and I'm tired already." His eyes shifted, a quick tentative glance she instantly understood, and returned, holding it just a little longer, then looking away.

"Yeah, I am too."

His laughter was faint, hesitant, slightly nervous. "I don't think I can drive too much farther."

Ahead the lights of the city were a white pyre lit in the blackness of the night, and she knew what he wanted and how to make it easy. "You shouldn't try. It could be . . ." just a catch and hint of emphasis, "dangerous."

She put the joint back on the edge of the ashtray and he took it from her before she could let go, his fingers touching hers, then pulling it to his lips. "I think I ought to go to a motel and get some sleep."

He did not look away from the road, but his mouth tightened, and his hands gripped the wheel harder, the bones straining under the skin, and she sighed, "Yeah, you ought to, but I guess I'll have to hitchhike on."

His question was as abrupt as a fumbled ball. "Why?"

"Wow, man, if I could afford to stay in a motel, I wouldn't have to hitchhike?

He did not allow himself to smile, the muscles in his face remaining motionless, but becoming harder, though his eyes grew brighter than the reflected glow of the city. She lay back against the seat, looking out through the polarized top of the windshield, watching the grayed stars, wondering if the life on those planets was as crazy and fucked-up as this, listening to him say, "I could get a room with twin beds, it wouldn't cost much more than a single this time of year. You could sleep in one and I could sleep in the other. You wouldn't have to ball me," taking another quick hit.

But his tone said, you don't have to ball me, but I want you to ball me, and she wanted to let him ball her because he wanted it, and it would make him happy, and she wanted him to be happy, and she said, "Wow, man, I could dig balling you."

He turned, eyes cold as waste. "Hey, chick, are you shining me?"

She shook her head, the ratted mass of her hair lying heavily behind her neck. "No, man, I could dig it."

"Okay," his voice was low, firm and intent as the town began in a strip of neon courts, flickering whiteredyellowblue, the signs an indecipherable collage of color, and she wondered, wrapped in silence while he looked for a motel, if she would come this time, or if only the presence of the aphrodisiacs had shattered the frigidity fear for that one wonderful profound climax, and she was now doomed to a life of gut cold indifference, if it could ever be indifference when you cared for someone, whether you came or not.

Only . . . when she thought of him, in this car next to her, and his prick, she remembered, without desire to remember or forget, that other him and that other prick in the shadowy lightshow of the church, on the yielding mirror floor that mirrored everything, and the memory of his face was the ultimate degradation, for it seemed as if, with the last spurting convulsion of his body, all her sins has been burned away, and she was free to start anew, a new life, a new person, both founded on the ashes of the old, and she resolved again, as she had resolved a thousand times in the two-and-a-half days since, not to lose sight of a single hard-earned lesson or a single hard-learned fact. And, maybe, in New York, when her head was straight, she would know what to do next.

But her thoughts, like a looped tape, fused into an endless repetition, kept returning to that moment on the floor in the dome when she had looked up into that face, the bleached hair almost reaching her own, the wind roughened flesh around his eyes tightening in a smile, tightening as it did that long ago morning of the day before on the monorail, when he held her steady as she lost her balance and fell to one knee and he helped her back up, his body pressing into hers, and she panicked and ran through the hot streets of the city, remembering, finally where she had seen him, and lying, arms and legs spread in repletion, his head on her belly, gasping the sweet downer-scented air, she raised herself, staring at his face, saying, "Hey, you're the guy from . .

"The monorail," he echoed, face abruptly alien with an emotion she had never seen. "The monorail where I planted the bug on the waist of your dress, Fuller," using the name no one could know, "or should I say Kovacks, Josette Kovacks; that was her name, remember, the girl you killed."

And terrified with a red pain fear as deep as her bowels, as wide as her guts, finer than any fuck she ever had, she gasped, "Who?" not really daring to know.

"Call it revenge, call it incest. Did you know she had a brother when you killed her?"

The   "Did you know she had a brother?"

shock   "Did you know she had a brother?"

of   "Did you know she had a brother?"

that   "Did you know she had a brother?"

moment   "Did you know she had a brother?"

still   "Did you know she had a brother?"

echoed, a solid physical ache in her chest, buried behind breasts and sternum. "Did you know she had a brother when you killed her?" he had asked and the world flashed one bright last time over the corpse of Andre Monkton Fuller, igniting the nova of Celeste Sladek, casting her forever from the slag metal of her body.

And now she lay back against the seat as his car grated across the asphalt drive of the motel, pulling to a stop before the office, the window lowering so he could shove his credit card in the "accounts" slot and thumb the "double" button, reading the cottage number from the lighted dial and taking the extruded plastic key. Then they drove along the white fronts of the houses to one near the end of the court, and came, coasting, to a halt, the engine dead, in the silence of the evening.

A bird trilled, sharp and clear, and she opened her door, not waiting for him, saving him the decision and the awkwardness, the click of his door following as he climbed out, dragging a suitcase down from the luggage rack, and walked around the car, the gravel of the path popping under his shoes, to unlatch the door. She went in after him, too weary to notice the room, crossing directly to the bed and falling on it, letting her body go and crashing into the spring-symphony of the mattress, thinking that it would be much nicer to do it in the morning after a shower, the first shower in four days, but that he would want to do it now, and she did not have the energy, now, to take a shower, and he had better be willing to accept her like this, dirt and all. But he ignored her and went into the bathroom, performing some masculine ritual she had no desire to understand, pissing, perhaps, or shaving, preparing himself for the night's promised coupling, never dreaming, or caring, why this girl, waiting for him to come out, was going to fuck him, only knowing that she was, and satisfied with that.

She stripped off the shift, soiled bra, and torn panties, folding them beside the bed and sliding under the covers, turning them down on the other side, and propping her head on a pillow, wondering why men always have to retreat into the john before each fuck, was it because they wanted to relieve their bladders so nothing would interfere with the sensations of their fuck, or did they just need a moment to commit themselves, fearing somehow the nitty-gritty contact with a woman? There was no way of really knowing, no way of crossing the barrier and being someone else, no way of truly understanding men, or, perhaps, even of understanding women. She would have to take them as they came and deal with them as they demanded, and let it go at that.

The door snicked open, derailing her train of thought, diverting it into the considered appraisal of his business-suited figure, rumpled, but not ever wrinkled, after the day's drive, face tense with anticipation, eyes eager and apprehensive, the apprehension of the sex game, the momentary insane fear of rejection, the dread of not being cared for, the need to have a woman care enough to fuck, the age old last minute uncertainty that is lost in the next step, no, not lost, but hidden behind a mask of assurance, a wall of confidence, hidden, wrapped, and safe in the farthest reaches of the mind, fearful of daylight and pain, but driving, powering, motivating everything else. She smiled, patting the bedcovers on the empty side, and leaned over the sheets falling away from armpit to waist, snapping off the lamp, leaving only the filtered radiance of the neon signs, sure that the brief glimpse of breast she had offered was enough encouragement to ease his nervousness.

The muffled sound of his shoes on the carpet crossed to the bed, and she saw him for just a moment, outlined against the window, looking at her with an expression she knew was doubtful, before he sat down, fully clothed, across from her. His hand moved over the covers, touching her ankle tentatively, then running smoothly up calf and thigh and hip and waist, ending very gently on her breast, and she reached out her arms, taking his shoulders and pulling him down, his head a dark shape lost in shadow, their lips meeting, her mouth opening to receive his tongue.

She slid her hands up around his back, fingers clasping, crushing him in the circle of her arms, mouth wet and willing against his, feeling the tension drain from his muscles as he caressed, softly, the hard tip of her nipple. His tongue came out of her mouth, flicking over the soft skin of her lips, and set fire to her neck, working, as she turned her head, to the ear, a wet penis-snake in the seashell convolutions of flesh, his breath a forge of intoxication, blowing through the passageways of the body, heating with a bellows heat, the banked embers of sexuality, kindling womb, vagina, and clitoris to an aching arousal.

She jerked his coat off, tangling the sleeves, wanting the velvet coppery touch of his flesh on hers, and he sat up, taking off sweater, undershirt, pants and shoes, flipping the covers over both of them and rolling next to her, his prick pushing into her navel through the fabric of his shorts. It was longer, when she reached her mouth out to his, running her tongue over his lips, her hand tracing the outline under the cloth, than she had expected, but thinner, width having, somehow, been transmuted into length, already throbbing faintly with the pressure of his semen, and she knew what she wanted to do

102

next, or thought she did until the feather touch of a tongue on her eyelids became an agony so sweet she forgot everything, and they seemed suspended in a timeless moment of gentleness, as if she had at last found her desperately sought peace with the world and were held, safely, outside the great war of life, and she understood that his hesitations had been those of a good man unused to casual lays and that he liked to care about women, and did care about them, and made love to them, as he was making love to her now, reverently.

When he let go, she kissed him a quick, lips together, kiss of affection, and tossed the covers off, twisting around, knees by his head, mouth poised above the slender column of his penis, rigidly pulling the waist of his shorts away from his flesh, and blew on it, slowly, watching it jump in the dim light. His hands touched her legs, tracing curlicue patterns over the fronts of the thighs, his breath stirring the electric wire bristles of her pubis, seeping through the crack of the lips into her cunt, and she brushed his covered prick with her face, the shaft rising up to smite her. One of his hands came down, dragging the shorts to his knees, and the inflamed head swung free, seeming to thrust forward with the beat of his blood, and her mouth dissolved, like the abrupt transition of an acid-trip, into an empty vessel moaning to be filled.

She flicked her tongue across the cleft of the corona, and as the breath whistled through his teeth into the pit of her vagina, she licked down along the sensitive foreskin, inching the shaft in past lips and teeth and palate to the entrance of the throat, tasting, in corkscrew spirals, the bland, salty flesh of his member, listening, smiling, to the sound of his lungs, to the reedy gasp of his moans. The heater clicked on, purring dimly beyond the roar of blood in her ears, and she drew away, sucking down the length of the prick, letting go with a smacking sound, turning to let him take her, drive himself into the center of her body, but he rolled onto her, hands pressing her hips into the bed, his head forcing itself between her thighs, and she lay back, arms outstretched, his prick against her face, letting his tongue worm its way into her crotch.

103

The engorged extension of her clitoris blazed with a heat greater than fire, and a sheet of yellow lightning arched from his mouth through her tissues, separating flesh from bone and bone from marrow, reducing her to bright hot ache of cunt and clit, a cavity tightening on itself, demanding the release of prick and fuck, needing him, with a flesh and bowel need, to drive his shaft into the willing rut of her body. But his tongue, impossibly, as long and as hot and as wet, plunging into the walls of her vagina, seemed to reach the very anvil of her womb, drawing her through the pores of her skin into the meatpackage of her body, dragging her down, at last, to the tempered serpent in her vitals.

She moaned, cried, screamed, pressing his head into the reeking furnace of her cunt, thrusting her hips against him, shrieking for him to go deeper and deeper, to lick the very retinas from her eyes, to touch her tongue, with his, from the bottom, to cleanse her body inside, as she wanted to cleanse his out, and she grabbed his prick with shaking hands, cramming it into her throat, sucking in and in until it seemed he must soon meet himself, rocking back and forth, breath forced past the plug of his member, the corona swelling, stopping her mouth with its immensity, and he jerked, with one last cry, his semen, heated beyond any concept of heat, splattering against throat and lips, and she swallowed convulsively, every spurt pouring down into her belly . . . but with his come, with his screaming, crying, moaning, shouting shuddering climax a barrier as cold as frozen steel slammed down across her hips, sealing her womb off behind a wall as thick as death, and she sobbed, holding herself to him in desperation.

If he knew she had not come, he never showed it, and later, when he let her off in Joplin, she could not remember his name.

2.

The room was small, dark and dirty, a heavy current of air seeping in through the windows beside the door around the corner from the parking section of a department store, it had a dull sour odor the texture of mold, and the walls seemed brittle with age, as if the building above had been constructed on the foundation of a more ancient one; like all revolutionary movements, she realized, this one met in dingy, inexpensive bars, as much because revolutions are for the disenfranchised, who have nothing to lose or to spend, as because the establishment never used them, and they could be taken over, en masse, by a small group. Through the top of the window-and-a-half, beyond the edge of the street, she could see a thin stretch of winter sky, chill and blue, remote as death, and watch the leaves boiling in the trees in New Central Park, but that was at the end of a narrow alley, and she turned back to the table, bringing her last Gold to her lips and lighting it, wondering when everyone else would get there and why she had felt sick the last two mornings.

Only one other guy had tried to make her on the road east, and she had let him, smiling at the great lover sweep them right off their feet swinger mask he used to hide his needs and insecurities, it was unimportant, his body shaking with release in her arms, that she didn't come; she didn't care, it was enough that he found what he needed, and that she could help him find it. The rest of the marathon, across the cotton states and up the shoulders of the Alleghenies to the coast, had been a sleepless procession of all night diners, gas stations, and dirt road stops, waiting for another lift, holding the aching arm out until someone remembered the old customs and offered a ride.

But in New York, in the dark roots of the city, it seemed worth it, and she found, on the first evening, that the people who walk, as a pastime, through the streets at night, are still the strange ones, the homeless, the seeking, and a girl with a

105

face as wistful as a flower, had come up, offering her a small chain of bells, saying, "You look lost." And she had answered, "Yes, I think I am," and the girl had taken her to a rotting sanctuary, the hulk of a pre-plague apartment house, and found her friends.

None of the guys had made any passes at her, and none of the girls either, they left her to her cubicle, in what had once been a walk-in closet, and made no more mention of her lack of sex life than they did of their own promiscuity. She would have let them, if they had, boys or girls, but no one tried, they were not concerned that someone did not want to fuck them, because someone did, and she had no desire to make love, only to comfort. They had taken her in, turned her on, and accepted her, she was free to do as she wished. They fed her until she found a job hand-weaving personal flags for decorations, and then charged her rent, none of them had any money, none of them cared or could afford to have any. They were all younger than she remembered having been, but not too much younger than she looked, and she felt decades older than them all. They lived at the forefront of a revolution, demanding the final logical changes from the world that had given them birth, and she felt, for some reason, close to them.

A bell rang over the door, jangling as it opened, and a crack shot across the room to the table where she sat, falling short at her feet, the tall figure of Killer coming in against the chill light, and she nodded as he took a seat opposite her, offering him a hit off the joint.

"Thanks," he said, sucking on the red coal, the paper burning and charring as it ate in, breathing his words out slowly, expending as little air as possible, trying to hold the smoke in his lungs. "I needed this. Been a really up tight day. I had to rap on everyone's head for the money, I have to have it into the agency by next Tuesday. Wow, I really didn't need that today."

His face was burned black, the lines around his eyes almost blistered, and his moustache drooped down beyond his chin, but the pupils were the black serpent quick of a poet and his hands were as nervous. She shook her head and said, "I can spare it, here's mine," pulling the money out of her purse and counting off the bills.

"Okay," he stuffed the money in a pocket of his kilt and crossed her name off a list, the heavy black line almost canceling the debts, and leaned back, the plastic chair creaking under his weight. "I guess they ought to be here soon." He glanced at his watch. "The weather must have slowed them down. The hail at noon was fierce."

She looked over the black tweed of his shoulder at the glacier cold, clear sky, wondering if the faint shadow on the north was the return of the scuttling clouds that had, off and on, choked the city for weeks, drenching it in rain, shattering it with hail, freezing it with snow gusts of wind. His hand reached out, rolling the cigarette between thumb and index finger, offering it back, the bones of his arm long and pronounced, the wrist sticking out of the sleeve of his coat, skin dark with ground-in dirt, but freshly washed, and she took it, dragging in, the grass crackling softly, and said, "I didn't even want to leave the house, but I had to deliver a special order to one of the shops, so I waited until the last minute and stopped here on the way back."

The chime over the door rang and her eyes flickered to it as he turned to look, but it was only Martine letting the cat out, and they both sighed, the distant rumble of thunder echoing against the windows.

"Evil day," he muttered, "evil. I wonder sometimes, if we, living together, turning on together, loving together, can't get along without bickering and hassles, then how can we demand the world make its final change and break out of its interim cocoon."

"Do you really think it will?" she asked, killing the joint in the ashtray.

He laughed, his mouth bending up, the deep sunken, ghost-hollows of his eyes softening, "You don't really care, do you, Celeste?"

"No," she shook her head. "I don't. I'm sorry."

107

The muscles of his face tightened into intent concentration, and he leaned forward, pupils dilating, compensating in the darkness.

"Hey, you don't have to be sorry. It just seems strange, that's all." He settled back in the chair, letting distance creep between them. "You already seem to know where it's at, or to be where it's at, without having to think. You seem to have a perception beyond consciousness, a direct confrontation between ego and reality."

"You seem to be a poet," she answered, reaching inside her blouse to ease the off-center constriction of a strap.

"I talk too much like one, you mean," he chuckled.

"You talk like what you are, is that wrong?"

"No," his long hair tossed out from the sides as he shook his head. "I can't very well complain about that."

Lightning flickered on the dark, aged walls, and the whole sequence, her being here, where she had come from, where she was going, the world that had produced these kids, the situation that made them meet here, in this kind of place, the attitude that made it possible for them to ignore it, all flashed, at once, a single thought, in her mind, and she said, "We all act like what we are, and we are all what we have been forced to be."

His brows knotted together, the dark hairs merging. "I'm not sure, exactly, what you mean."

"Oh God," she thumbed a button, feeding change into the slot beside it, and a Coke dropped into the gate at the edge of the table, "it's so simple, I don't know how to explain it." The plastic cover stuck and she had to slit it with her fingernails before she could get it open. "I haven't thought about it much."

"What do you think about, Celeste?"

"People," she answered, sipping away the foam. "It's warm."

He craned his head. "Martine! Your goddamned refrigerator's not working again."

The owner ducked his head and faded into the wiring system of the restaurant, the door opening and closing again, a damp blast of air filtering through. "It really is hard to explain."

108

"What's hard to explain, Celeste. Hi, Killer," a short blonde girl, not quite plump, sat down next to her.

"I think, if she ever gets a chance," his voice was heavy with sarcasm, "she is going to explain what makes people tick."

"Oh, dry up, Killer," the girl said. "I haven't done anything yet."

"To who?" he asked, staring down at her, tearing the top off a pack of Panama Reds.

"To anyone, yet," she pushed a button and, coffee fell into the receiving gate.

"That's unusual for you, Sappho."

"Frig you—"

"—you dug it, remember?"

"—I want to hear Celeste," she said, ignoring him.

Rain shattered between the narrow slats of the catwalk and ran in wavery sheets down the windows. The guttural hum of the dehumidifier increased, a smooth steady sound, the sound of wind on leaves. A familiar ease blanketed her, the echo of childhood. She remembered telling Howard how it had affected her, the night before the marriage, and now the wind had reached her here, sweeping through all those years, and she pressed the stick-tight tabs of her jacket together, sealing out the chill, sorting among the chaotic fragments of impression for the right words.

They were watching her, Killer and Sappho, full-fleshed blonde and dark poet, waiting for her to speak, willing to give her time to make any decision, find any words, unconcerned by time or place, interested only in what she had to say, and she had, yet, nothing to say, but the words were forming in the torrent cavern of the subconscious, on the threshold of consciousness, and Sappho still held the unlit joint in her hand. "Aren't you ever going to light that thing?"

"Yeah, wow," she reached down into the pocket of her stockings, and pulled out a book of matches. "Here," she set it aflame, blew out the flame, took a hit, and passed it on.

The smoke was dry and pungent, the flavor of cloves baked by sunshine, and she drew it slowly, parting lips around the tip to cool it with air, into the bellows-foundry of her lungs, handing the cigarette to Killer, letting the resins coat pleura and trachea . . . "Well," the exhalation was faint, almost clear, "I think it's this way," the stone rolling into her skull. "Take you, Killer," his head lifted, the eyes glittering in the deep pits of the sockets, "you're a poet," he smiled ironically and half-bowed across the table, "underneath, and a clown," the surface of his face, muscles and skin, went slack a moment, and then he drew them slowly into a grotesque expression, eyes crossed, "on the surface, theatrical, anyway, and, of course, sharp in business," his free hand drummed once, the fingernails, one by one, clacking against the plastic table top, "though you almost never use it, still you keep the Sanctuary running. I won't discuss your brains," he blew her a kiss, giving the joint to Sappho, "brains are independent of character, like pie, as a kind of food, is independent of any particular filling you use in it."

"Only a broad would think of an analogy like that," he said, and she saw him seeing her as a girl, as a woman, doing all the girlwoman things, baking, sewing, fucking, his conception of her based on a reality that had never existed, attempting to reach, with a poet's vision, an insight he could never find.

"But what caused you to become what you are, what caused any of us to be what we are? The answer's a kind of reciprocal development of strength and weakness, the weakness causing the growth of the strength to protect it, hide it, mask it, defend it, and the two becoming independent facets of each other."

Her own words were bright flame points, leafflowers of the stoneblossom growing on the bonetrellis convoluted skull, hanging in the eyecenter of inner-vision, and the three-dimensional light-warmed figures at the table, multiplied by two during the self-blinded charge of her thoughts, were peripheral reflections barely visible, dimly understood. Someone, Sappho, short pale hair meeting in the point of a crusader's helm beneath her chin, held out the redyellow stub of the cigarette, a burning offering, and she took it, the sudden rush entry of the grass highlighting the pastel colors of the

110

words, images, memories boiling up from the burst files of the subconscious into daylit clarity.

"You're really heavy tonight." Sappho's voice, the whispered incantation of an infidel priest, brought her back to the beginning of the thought chain.

"What made you a poet?" Their eyes met, even flush, set far back beneath the occipital bones, they met, his flat and wary, waiting, waiting . . . and she went on, not really having paused. "Pain, pain and fear. You hurt, the world hurt you. Maybe you were already a little strange, a little more aware, a little more intelligent. Enough to be thought different, enough to be treated different. Everyone knows when they're being treated different. They feel it, no matter why, as a sense of isolation, of rejection. They feel left out, not, and they aren't a part of the regular world everyone else lives in. That hurts, man."

The joint was back in her hands, did that mean they were smoking fast or she was talking slow, she couldn't tell, and took another hit, but never her eyes off his, cowering or triumphant in their shadowy sockets, his face a mask, like all other masks, no thicker than the porelayer of skin, but impenetrable, and one of them, one of the two who had come in, said in the distant annoying buzz of a fly, "Wow, she must really be stoned tonight. I don't think I've ever heard her say this much in all the time she's been here," but it flashed from her ears to her brain, never rippling her consciousness.

"You have to look at things, not as isolated phenomenon, but as part of a series, linked and self-reinforcing. Look, when people treat you differently than they do everyone else, you feel, correctly, left out, apart. But being apart, you are able to see them, and their workings, from the outside, objectively, something you could never do if you were accepted as part of their group. And if they didn't hurt you, however unintentionally, and you always feel rejected and hurt by being treated differently, you would never feel anger. Take anger and viewpoint, they always produce insights no one in a group could have, and the anger always demands that the insight express itself."

111

Killer took a long, long, long hit, looking at her, glitteringly. "I give you the poet," his voice mocked. "Insight and anger," but the muscles of his face were tighter than drawn steel.

"I think," Sappho said, "she's right. You are great because you are a poet, all it takes to be a poet, but you are a poet because you were, and maybe still are, hurt and afraid and alone, and out of that has come you."

But his eyes never left hers, never went to Sappho, never glanced in greeting at the two who had joined them, but only stared into hers, and she wondered if she had gone too far, said too much, wounded too deeply, wounded him at all, when all she had wanted to do was explain because he had wanted to know, and she hadn't meant any of it. Thunder shook the air around them, a ghost light in the windows, sliding from sky to earth and gone, leaving an aftertaste of copper, the sweet tang of ozone on her tongue; his tongue, passing beyond the edge of his teeth, distorted the thin line of the underlip, and, darkly, glistened in the opening hollow of the mouth.

"Shall I recite, from pain and fear and loneliness, a poem?" he asked, a pinpoint of brightness, brighter after the lightning than before, bordered by concentric glowing rings; reflected through the gray haze of smoke, dancing on the surface of his pupil; the sum of desperation, chalky flesh tight across the cheekbones, inclination of head, fingers hard and loose in deliberate relaxation, hidden from everyone but her by shadow and angle.

She smiled, trying to bridge the gap from mind to mind with a spark of caring so he could see, and have no doubt, that she had never, even if she had, meant to threaten him or to hurt him, and if he wanted it, as forfeit or in comfort, he could have her body as the proof. But he looked into her, through her, past her, and refocused on some private vision, his body, clothed, in repose, working, with every muscle, to force the words out.

"Celeste; a cycle
A darkness
turning into light
a smile

112

brighter than
a star
a far
distant
vision
in a night
strewn
with the
embers
of embattled
sorceries
and kings
whose bright
swift
armor
failed
wrecked
on an altar
of happiness
unable
to contain
within
the fires
of ecstasy."

The star field of his eyes, snared in the black net of his face, came back to hers, poised, fumbling on the edge of some insane flight, ready to flee from too heavy a touch, and she reached out, gently, her hand to his, fingers trapped around interlaced fingers, squeezing them and holding his gaze, meeting and sustaining the whiteheat intensity, trying to understand.

"Thank you," she said.

"That's a cycle?" Sappho snorted.

His face turned through a jump-frame discontinuity where the filmstrip motion of reality had been broken and spliced back, feet apart, reached here, by her attempt to reach him, and, still wondering as the vibrations and then the meaning of Sappho's voice penetrated, he began to . . . turn, but not the same face at all, a different, friendly, social face, a special for

Sappho and the other face, but not the face she had, for a moment, touched.

"It's the start of a cycle."

Sappho snorted, draining her coffee, making a face at the bitter, powder dregs. "Where are the rest?"

The muscles of his face pulled his lips back against his face in a feral grin. "I haven't written them yet."

"Why?" Sappho's hand tossed the hair from face, letting it fall back behind her shoulders, and lightning drew a gray film across all their figures.

But the inertia of the stone clung to the gaunt shadows of Killer's face, and Celeste watched, held, the interplay of light and dark, the subtle tension of conscious and unconscious expression across his flesh. Beaded sweat, rolling down the oily skin, formed around the freshly-shaven stubble of his beard, and his throat bobbed with the motion of a half-finished swallow she understood only too well.

She said and He said in practically the same tone at practically the same time, but his words seemed to echo hers, and she had, after all, been fast enough, saying, "Because, I think, he hasn't known me long enough—"

"Because," with a poet's honesty, no matter what. "I haven't known her long enough—"

"—and that's the first."

"—and that's the first one. There'll be more, later."

The golden dome of Sappho's hair flared out in negation. "Why don't you ever write any about me?" The cold blue of her eyes was almost hungry.

He laughed, the dead memory of the lightning kindled in his face. "Because you aren't, to a poet, not a man, as fascinating. There's an infinite depth, a subtle mystery to Celeste. The eternal female."

The eternal female, did the ghost of Andre Fuller stir, slumber disturbed, or was it only her own sense of the sublime and the ridiculous, newly found and very near the surface? She had been, because she had to be, seeing in every lonely face and every desperate glance the reflection of her own torment, as careful and attentive to them as she could find it in her . . .

heart? to be. Was that, after all, what men saw as the truly feminine?

"I don't know," Sappho said, shaking her head, "there must be something dirty somewhere."

General laughter.

In spite of everything a cold wash of rain filtered through hair and cap and trickled inside the back of her coat collar, and she shivered, though the metal pilings of the wharf, caught the night wind. A faint sea phosphorescence carpeted the sand, and, with the city behind them, only the ocean was dark, dark and rhythmic, the grumbling tide mingling salt and rain on her lips. Farther down, where the omnipresent activity of the docks filled the sky with a funeral glow, she could see the figures of workers crawling over the unsteady decks of the ships, but here, on the far curve of the harbor, only the five of them and the dying starfish moved.

The pencil beam of Killer's Hash picked out the way before them, and she kicked a can out of her path, listening to it skitter out of sight; and the wind off the steel beams was like the rush of the wind through the leaves in her childhood, the sound of the wind off the hood of a car on the Los Angeles freeway, the penetrating comfort of the wind between the worlds.

"What you have said," Sappho began, "is not just that we are products of our environment, but that what we are, good and bad, is a development, an extension of what we have been. That good and bad grow at the same time out of each other, that the good is a compensation for the bad, can only exist, at first, because of the bad, and that, maybe, the bad is only our attempt to protect the ego and strike first."

"Say it this way and forget it; good and bad are only different facets of the same personality, only different perspectives on the same thing."

"I can't forget it, it fits in with the tideflow of consciousness across this continent."

Killer swung his light across her face, showering amber highlights through her damp hair.

"Now who's the poet?"

115

"All of us are, these days." A gnarled trunk of driftwood shouldered up from the sand, and Sappho smoothed out her cherry-leather skirt, settling against it, lighting another joint.

"I think we're in for a marathon rapping number," someone sighed, but their bodies were only vague blurs in the undershadow of the pier.

Sappho's hands moved defensively across the slope of her lap, tangling and working free, the nervous, strobed gestures of a gold stone. "Now it isn't that bad."

Gravel popped, leather cased boots on rock, and Celeste turned, accepting the hand stretched out in the dark and sinking to her knees, leaning her head on the proffered bulk of a shoulder. "Thanks, Killer."

The cigarette changed hands, passing around the circle, and Sappho waited for it to return, dragging in before she spoke, the words dribbling out, "That's not really old-fashioned one-two—three logic thinking, that's a new kind of thinking altogether, and it takes a new kind of consciousness."

A sardonic voice hooted out of the night, "You're shining me on."

Beneath her cheek the muscles of his arm bunched, then relaxed, and his breath half-caught, almost undetectable, the calculus of desire; she rubbed her head against the wool of his jacket in acceptance, squeezing his shoulder.

"It started and ended here. Follow this series of logic, from thinking in instantly envisioned sets of things, always looking at the thought, the word, from as many different viewpoints as possible, while thinking it," she gulped."Take television and the leisure class, the technology to produce the one rested on the technology to produce the other, whichever way you look at it. Series logic, remember? The leisure was not for a few, but for literally everybody, even the ghetto workers had a few hours at night to watch TV.

"Like, before, all the average man had to or could know was his little situation, plot of earth, city apartment, his job or how to till the land, and he returned home, with, maybe, twelve hours before he had to return to work, twelve on or twelve off, too exhausted to do anything but sleep."

116

"Rap on blonde witch," Killer whispered.

"Even, with almost no communication over distance, those who had time and wanted to learn had little information to hold in their head. But came the leisure class and television.

"Everyone had time to be entertained, and, when they weren't working, wanted to be, and they had television, a medium of nearly instantaneous communication. Even the dumb classics, the western and detective and adventure shit, had to have some small background in the world, had to contain some slivers of facts.

"So, from having a very little to learn and no time to learn it, man went to having a great deal thrust at him and time to sit before it. By nineteen sixty-six, when the revolution began to be felt, the average child in his teens knew as many facts as Einstein had ever learned.

"The demands had been changed and the systems of consciousness, the techniques had to be changed to fit. They had been geared to the demands of a people who only took in a small amount of data, they had never been designed for more. A new kind of consciousness had to develop, a way of dealing with infinitely more knowledge in a lifetime than had ever been needed before.

"You see, the children who grew up with television, after the bomb, after forty-what'sit, had to have developed a new kind of consciousness, one that could cope with the world they grew up in and its communication of ideas.

"But any revolution in consciousness will become a revolution in a system no longer geared to it, and nothing remains unquestioned, the old order passeth. And the system cannot communicate with them or influence them, because all its methods of persuasion and communication were designed by and geared to old style consciousness. If they wondered why all their tactics failed and then perished, it was because a man who knows very little and is used to knowing very little, can easily be lied to, but a man who has learned a hundred contradictory things will take nothing unquestioned. People were no longer easily fooled, youth were not as limited in their thinking as youth had been before.

117

"Everything from the revolution against the war to the revolution against bigotry all stemmed from the revolution in consciousness, the automatic instant re-reexamination of everything, the ability to look at things from several different viewpoints at once, all new ways of assimilating data. The old lies were out. They were out from the moment anyone said why, and said it, and said it, and said it, always aware of how big the unknown was, never taking because for an answer.

"Part of the new consciousness was an acid-trip afterawareness, on a gut-deep level, where it had never reached, a direct personal experience of man's brotherhood, that all men are basically alike, a vision of man as godhead, all resulting from the acid need to expand and a medium that showed a man what he could never have seen before, thousands on thousands of other men, all living differently, all determined that they were right. It became more than words in a book, it was a reality that shook all foundations. They wanted freedom and they were willing to trust others with it. Old laws had to go.

"The restrictive ones went, the ones that protected people from themselves, abortions became legal, drugs became legal, weapons became legal, pornography became legal, homosexuality became legal, freedom became legal.

"The system changed, its ways of dealing with people changed to fit the requirements of the new people it would have to deal with, the educational system changed to deal with a consciousness that required new techniques in teaching.

"It took revolution, though, physical revolution. It always does, no establishment ever yields unless it's forced to. The haves never change because of words. It takes force. Why should I change the things that are good for me merely because you want it? Words will never pry what is mine from me, only action.

"Too brutal?

"The Negro was a second-class citizen of this country for over a hundred years, and no amount of words, however logical or eloquent, could change that. But when they put a gun to the head of the old system, it was, 'Yes, sir, how much would you like and when?' Of course, without television to show the Negro what he was missing and, in every show, flaunt before him what was the accepted norm in living so far above him, it would have taken longer for him to catch fire. It happened after television came, remember?

"For years students, television-fed students, cried out against an educational system designed by and for men in whose lives only a little information could come, and no one listened. 'It was good enough for us, kid, shut up.' But the kids they were speaking to were used to knowing that there is always more to know, and could not even understand that kind of answer. But they were ignored, until they seized the schools and set them ablaze. Then it was, 'Yes, sir, how much change would you like, and when?'

"But the capper, the end of the system, was the Humphrey–Nixon nomination. It was so hollow, no one knew for sure what the differences, if any, in their platforms were, or even what their platforms were. Nixon was a nebbish, a nice guy, a nothing. Humphrey, besides having sold out his original position to become vice-president and keep the chance to become president, was obviously, on record, not the choice of the people of the Democratic party for candidate. Fuck, even in his home state, he couldn't get enough votes in the primaries to come knee high to . . . what's his name."

"McCarthy," Killer whispered.

"McCarthy. But they ignored what the people wanted, thinking the liberals would eat any shit that had the tag 'Democratic Party' on it They thought the old lies would do, as they had always done. How could they suspect or control a new kind of consciousness?

"It was the last election with no freedom of choice. Riots for four years, killing for four years, death for four years, war and plague and pestilence. But the television generation came into its own, and the world changed."

"Poet," someone challenged.

"Fuck you," Sappho replied, and moved away from the tree. "Come on, I'm going home.'

White sand spumed beneath their feet as they ran down the graveyard-silent beach, and the wind whipped it sharp and cold, into her face. Overhead gulls wheeled against a ragweed sky, the stars, behind the tissue clouds, were frosted, and the air in her lungs was a ragged pain. Laughter followed them, Killer in front, Sappho almost at his side, the rest trailing, the laughter behind.

She had loosened the collar of her jacket and the cold edged down across her chest, the silent pounding of her boots lost in the roar of the ocean. Killer flung the stilt-work shadow of his body to the ground and rolled over, back powdered white, grinning at the sky. The others fell around him, dark birds on a darker strand, all except Sappho, who stood, poised, wild with the sound of her own laughter.

"Come on, you can't quit here," she cried. "Celeste, don't give up," her voice edged with an unuttered plea.

They held for a moment, surrounded by a night of poetry, stoned and expectant, the swift rush of a wave breaking in her, a net of hair whipping across her eyes as she watched the blonde girl, waiting, both waiting, both watching the other watch, and she saw the many splendored wheel of need revolve before her, the dark cavern of a poet's face, the intent desperation of Sappho's mouth, the unfettered freedom of the beach, the unfettered freedom of now, converging, and she made her peace with the war of life, and broke, racing, past the startled shadows of the men, down the shining path of sand.

The moon followed, flickering behind railed clouds, a crosspatch pattern of night and day as painful to her eyes as sunlight, and she let them jar shut with each step, and open, and shut, and open, a bewildering landscape of half-second images, piled one upon the other, until, at last, they came, gasping, to the base of a cliff, the gray stone rising into darkness.

"Shall we go back?"

"Do you think they've waited?"

"I doubt it."

"They knew?"

"They suspected."

' "Well, what shall we do then?"

"Coffee is usual, I think."

"Lovely."

And it was as simple as that, she had to do no more, and they went, hand in hand, into the streets

"Do you think it will rain again?"

"It's winter."

"You're right."

"Killer is cool."

"Very cool."

"I've slept with him."

"I haven't."

"He's really very lovely."

"He's a good man."

"I've wanted you a long time."

"I'm glad."

'I wish right now. . . ."

"But first — "

" — Coffee?"

"Right," she answered, the door sucking

as she broke the light beam, letting Sappho in before her, holding the light on her hand and the doors apart.

The long narrow restaurant was, even after midnight, crowded, the booths overflowing with the gross national product of people and dinnerware. Gilded steel beams ribbed the roof, pressing down on the eyes, and the silverfish of reflected light swam in the windows. There was no waitress in sight and she wondered if they were to seat themselves, nothing here was like California, and it was hard to tell where mechanization left off.

"There," Sappho pointed to an empty table far down the right wall, and Celeste followed down the antiseptic brightness of the room.

"I'll get it," she said, covering Sappho's payment slot with her hand. "I sold a flag today and I'm flush."

White teeth bit into a pale underlip, nodding. "Okay," and a sheen of gold rippled over polished hair. "I'm close to broke, anyway."

"I think I'll have something to eat."

"Like what?"

"Dessert."

"Peanut butter cream pie."

"Ugh."

"No, really, it's very lovely."

"Well. . . ."

Her mouth was warm and wet and red, the lips soft, the tongue restless in the bellcavern of the throat; her eyes were blue, swirling in and out of focus, now sharp and hard, bright and intent, now tender, lit with the warmth of desire; her hair curved in, bracketing her cheeks, meeting below the point of the chin: a crusader's helm.

"If Killer is the poet, does that make you a philosopher?"

"Sarcasm?"

"Curiosity."

"You're a funny girl."

"I didn't mean it that way."

"All right."

"But you're funny, just the same. Passive."

"Passive?"

"The world passes by and you watch. You react. You don't do things. You react to them."

"Okay."

"It's true. Killer saw that."

"His poem?"

"Don't toss it off. He doesn't often do poems about people he knows well."

"Does he know me well?"

"Don't be coy."

"I didn't mean to be."

"But you're hard to know. You go along with almost everything: start nothing."

"I like to watch things."

"All you do is watch."

"I like to watch."

"But that's all you do."

"I learn."

"I don't understand you."

"I'm —"

"And don't say, you're sorry."

"But you were right."

"About what?"

"Television and us."

"Well, don't let that mislead you. I'm not smart."

"Did you pick it up from someone else?"

"No, not exactly. But it's obvious."

"No one else thought so."

"They were stoned."

"Stoned, not stupid."

"Look, it wasn't that hard to think of. The facts were like the spokes of a wheel; one day they came together at the center, that's all."

"The new kind of thinking, huh?"

A grin. "You got me."

"I know."

Firefly lights glimmer on the triple prongs of forks and steam rises from an earthenware mug on a Formica-surfaced table top like the formation of a genie from an enchanted bottle.

"You never talk about your past."

"I have no past."

"You don't want to talk about it?"

"I just have no past."

"You don't remember it?"

"I just don't have one, that's all."

"Well . . . all right . . . but you can't have been born yesterday."

"No, I wasn't born yesterday."

"Only, I wonder about you, we all do."

"There's nothing to wonder about, really."

"Everything seems to go into you, nothing seems to come out."

"I don't know what you mean."

"You're so passive. About everything."

"I like to watch things happen."

"It's more than that. I think if one of the boys had asked you first, you'd have gone with them."

"I would."

The pupil may have narrowed, it may not, but Sappho's eyes seemed darker with the depth of thought, her face a living flesh-mask short-circuited, still connected to the person underneath, and, no, not pain, but bewilderment, twisted through it on the interface level between muscle and skin.

"You are surprised?"

"Yes."

"But you've slept with a man."

"Many men."

"Then what?"

"It's your face."

"My face?"

'It is so untouched, virginal."

"You thought I was a virgin?"

"No, but I thought . . . that you were unused to sex, unused to men . . . you have the softness of a woman who is used to women."

"Yes, you could say that."

"That you've known women."

"That I've known women."

"I thought as much."

"But you interest me more."

"I do?"

"Yes."

"How?"

"You say the thought came to you by accident, the facts on the rim of a wheel, suddenly converging at the hub?"

"Yes."

"I think you are too modest. I think you are brilliant."

"I've often thought so."

"Seriously."

"Okay, seriously."

The flat reflective surface of the table separated them, a rectangle of space isolating them, not quite visible but thick and viscous, a faint resistance to communication building a tension they both could feel.

"What next?"

"Us?"

"No, what happens next with the world?"

"More revolution."

"More?"

"The rest, if you will. The part they weren't ready for."

"Why not?"

"They grew up with television, but they were raised by people who didn't, conditioned by a world set in the old pattern."

"And we were raised by them?"

"Yes."

"And we are freer, newer, closer to the new image than they are?"

"Yes."

"And we are ready for what they were not?"

"Yes."

"I see."

"Don't you see, though. They had too many hang ups left, were too conditioned still, were caught in a gap. They were only ready for more freedom, not total freedom."

"And we are?"

"Close to it."

"And now?"

"Total freedom. All laws have to go. There no need for law, not anymore."

"No?"

"No, not anymore. Not, anyway, by the time we destroy it."

"How will we live then?"

"That's really unimportant, don't you see. We will find a way, create a new society. We can cope with freedom, no one could do that before."

"I hope you're right."

"Don't you see that I am?"

The intent contraction of the pupil, the swan's breath tremor of expectancy, the abrupt leap of a pulse throbbing in the throat.

"I guess so."

"You'd go along with anything, wouldn't you?"

"Not anything."

"Anything that didn't upset you."

"I guess."

"And you don't upset easily?"

"No."

"Wanta go?"

"Yeah."

"Let's get out of here."

They were in the older section of the city, at the roots of the metropolis, surrounded by dirt-eaten piles of marble and brass, hemmed in by cracked and flaking mosaics of orange and green tile, the pale shimmer of the moon glared back from the metal casings of the windows. The sound of rats and dogs and cats prowling the garbage ways of the alleys echoed with their steps from the worn facades of the buildings, a flat, tinny telephone sound. She could not remember if they were coming or going, they had been prowling through the deserted level of the streets for hours, sometimes sitting on iron-lace railings talking, sometimes riding the darkened elevators of empty buildings, sucking down the stone laden smoke, surrounded by motion, pure motion, no light or sound or feel, only motion, drunk on the exhilaration of rising, as gods, to the sky. But, now, exhaustion crept up around them, filling the space between with silence, and Sappho moved closer, taking her hand, holding it as they walked.

Chill, dark air stabbed into her chest, and she coughed, throat closing and then ripped open with the explosion of breath.

"Are you all right?"

"Yes."

"You don't sound too good."

"No, really."

"Better take a cold pill when we get back."

"Soon, maybe?"

"Soon. But if you don't feel — "

"No, I'll be okay. It's just the dampness."

"Okay. It's just a little farther."

"Are we going someplace?"

"You'll see."

"I thought we were just walking."

"Well . . . we were and we weren't."

"Hmm?"

"There's something I want to show you. Then we'll see."

"All right."

Even the street lights were lost in the heavy winter mist blowing around them, thickening at their feet and crawling, inch by inch, up their legs. The sidewalk narrowed and vanished, leaving them on an old brick pavement, skirting the edges of puddles, crowded together by the arm's breadth nearness of the store fronts. A gull cried, sharp and keen on the night wind; the salt scent of the sea came to them for a moment and was gone.

Then the warehouses pressed in, funneling them down an alley narrower than a crack and they emerged on the lighted lawn of a park, before a building taller than the sky. It ran, ribbons of fluorescent color, half-a-hundred stories from the earth, circled by bands of opal balconies, set in a terraced garden of jasmine and rose. She ran forward to the street lights and clung, looking up and up until it seemed her neck would snap with the effort and it rose up still.

"They started an industrial park here when they decided to re-build New York on the other side of the river, but by the time they had voted on it and gotten started, all the city was becoming New York, and the center had shifted down to the bank."

"You mean it's empty, like some great and echoing tomb?"

"Well, no, not exactly. But not very many people have offices in it, and there're no guards at night."

Wonder burst, like a roman-candle, scarlet and emerald in her chest. "None?"

"Well, practically, he comes by at midnight, two, and four. It's two-fifteen now."

She spun, the weight of her hair settling back across the shoulders, and Sappho was beside her, jacket tight across the weight of her breasts, leaning toward her, and they stood, Sappho's eyes glittering blue, hard as stone, bright with fever.

"Let's go up."

"Good."

The grass was silver with rain and they cut across it, boots leaving black footprint shapes behind, coming to the gray glass immensity of the door. It opened for them and inside was a fairyland of wrought-iron webberies climbing the hollow circular center, disappearing in the upper dark, and they ran to the nearest open-trellised elevator, slamming the gate and pushing the buttons.

The dark button on the farthest column the highest floor

"Dark?"

"Dark."

The silent plate that banishes light

"Slow?"

"Slow."

The black knob the whine of a declining motor

Alchemy of stone changes of grass lampshades of yellow the intermeshed surface of skin and light shadow patterns diamonds the metal work cage goes up the skeletal framework down the shadow flows across her face across the intermeshed surface of skin and light across chin and mouth and nose and eyes and they swim it is the motion of waves waters shimmers dark water shimmers in the engulfed darkness of the cage her head tilts back golden helm opens light glints on the surface of her eyes her throat is full and strong well fleshed there is a dimple in the hollow of her throat she is waiting but not waiting her face is calm in repose still but she is tense the tension lies beneath her skin reflected in her eyes her breasts are fair haired full against the quilted fabric of the jacket the cloth is dark green and shiny thick her skirt stretched indents below the last protrusion of crotch a faint pool of shadow her breath is silent the hair hangs back

128

unmoving   a tiny crack of dark between the lips issuing the dying whisper of a breath

her face is moving forward against the current · of shadows they are a mask woven round her head   her eyes are lost in them   the points of the helm swing together shutting   the line of her mouth is shut   the lips sealed together by moisture and fear   the dark haired girl who died on the night of August eighteenth   face twisted in fear   eyes frozen in an outer vision · seeing what she had never wanted to see   the blonde beautician with that extra spark of woman   woman hunger   playing the oldest word game of all   Sappho   visions of Levantine beauty dark   sultry · clothed in gold and veils   seated upon pillows of silk and fur   waiting blonde   hungry crying to be loved   leaning forward   each downy hair on the upperlip gleaming   threads of gold   arms beginning to follow the motion of the head   when lip is on lip   they will encircle the waist   the skin tickle of an errant hair

lip is on lip   lip meets lip   lip touches lip   lip opens on lip mouth opens on mouth   tongue rushes against tongue   the strain of contact is sweet   bearable   soft   gentle   her tongue searches hungry seeks reassurance firm   denies its own need but is the warm pebbly slick fleshy reality of a human tongue soft as only a woman can be soft   sliding over the lubricated cavern of the mouth   hesitant   touching each new domain lightly   waiting   finding no refusal   taking it with harshness denying the hesitancy   firm now   existing as victor by acquiescence   a pretense fooling no one but her ego   a silence agreeing to her   victory the hot velvet of her flesh   the pressure of her arms   binding   leather skirt taut over wide hips   the flare of the pelvis wide   all mother the vastness of the birth channel easy   the hard grinding of the pubic symphysis   wasted all wasted   on answering female flesh   no consummation   release but no consummation   breast on breast   later nipple upon nipple   even belly against belly   vaginas wracked   wombs aching   pearls inflamed   release but no consummation

breasts   why   to be swollen with milk   belly   why to be swollen with child   womb   why   to receive the seed   vagina why   to receive the prick   nipples   why   to suckle the child

129

arms why to enfold both arms under hers beneath the
shoulderblades holding her kissing her kissing the wasted
flesh of her woman's body letting her have what she needs so
she too may make her peace with the war of life letting her
hide in the conquered comfort another body letting her need
purge sins she cannot imagine

a breath forces its way past the saliva coated obstruction of
her tongue cinnamon sweet moist lips close shut retreat slip
away into the shadow waters trailing away a last whisper she
stands head cocked staring eyes vanished in wells of darkness
the wave motion of her hair rebounding reverberating still
swinging kneels sinking sinking to the carpet the car is rising
slowly but rising rising through the cannonades of shadow
rising past the fairy sculpture of the landings rising against the
black bulk of the floors rising up a fifty stories tall opening the
wrought iron trellises of the cage quiver shake she is sitting
just off her legs on her knees her breasts swell under the
quilted fabric of the jacket fall she tilts her head back up hair
swinging open eyes climbing into the light the light mirror
white across pupils flashing waiting arms at sides palms on
floor waiting supplicant not able to admit entreaty naked
eyeflicker clothed but naked moving aside to make room
tongue flicking over lower lip breathing silently carefully
enjoining silence hands outstretched helping to peel off a
blouse make a pillow it

her weight arms and shoulders working out of the jacket
comes first against the knees and thighs and waist and chest
her mouth is hungry hungry for lips and throat and breasts
her hands are gently at the hook of the bra and palm under
cup of thigh mouth carrying away just before it the bra on
nipple on fire agony of breast tightness of womb wall against
wall against wall against wall against wall empty aching wet
and willing the ripple patterns of the waves wash down the
cage sinking into the darkness of the floor her face is darkness
all dark bent over the rounded shape of a breast half
shadowed the glint moisture of the tongue occasionally hand
beyond that running hair light down the inner slope of a thigh
brushing inside the skirt brushing out fingers swooping back

hiking up the skirt catching in the nylon panties jerking down the edge of a nail razor sharp

she rears up body bent back aflame with light and whirls down mouth seeking the pearl the clit her legs flashing out and open dark in the tunnels of the skirt and comes down the wet slick brush clam dark and moist yielding at the flicker of a tongue moaning open both mouths moaning open middles separated by thicknesses of cloth cores split open by the assaults of Orpheus flesh crying for the dagger quick intrusion of a tongue pierced piercing back she rolls aside weight to the floor of the car back mouth to mouth releasing bras and skirts bringing flesh to flesh

flesh to flesh warm flesh round flesh firm flesh freckled amber wholesome flesh breast against against breast weight transmuted not down but out to the side not weight but pressure her hand moves tracing a profile from hairline down cheek across lips along throat over breasts skimming ribs teasing navel brushing pubis stroking thigh returning to cheek imprisoning soft prison lips above flowering tongue striking against tongue steel against flint spark against spark igniting throat and crotch her back is smooth to the cleft of the hips her nipples erect the dimple in the hollow of her throat empty waiting to be filled with kisses kissed she cries fingers clenching in shoulder and arm writhes pelvis grinding on pelvis skin stretching tight across clitoris released teased and released again her hand slips between two legs seeming to sweep her own aside slides down the channel of the cunt caresses the pearl seeks entry of the womb the walls of the vagina reach out part suck it in both fingers and in and in and out racing and in and out the rhythm of her fingers somehow the rhythm of all lungs quick and hard

the rhythm becomes a need the vagina inflamed only her fingers easing it full in and inflaming it as they withdraw her tongue in the same rhythm a concerto of violence across the inflamed tip of the nipple fast and slow light and heavy broad and narrow wet and dry agony and ecstasy fire above and fire down below reaching out to her fingers taking them straining against them holding making of her flesh a banquet

131

the pressure of belly   the pressure of thigh   the flower scented
holiness of enfolding   her face lifts   soft and passionate   crusted
with sweat   body dripping with sweat   drop by drop   falling
the elevator rising   the agony   higher and higher   and higher
chords unresolved.

Celeste moaned   the cage sighing to a stop   hanging a
moment then starting down   down through the shadows   a
slow plunge through space   twisting the other girl under her
forcing her down   forcing her hand out   writhing   licking the
salt taste from ear   and throat   and breast   and stomach   and
navel   and hip   and spine   and the curling matted hairs of the
crotch   reaching the oysterish taste of the vagina   sliding
among the pinkish folds of flesh   smelling the final metallic
odor of a woman   seeking the root of the clitoris   tongue racing
over thick convoluted flesh   spreading the legs farther and
farther apart   opening the great funnel to the pit bottom light of
the elevator   touching the pimpled bottom of the pearl   hearing
her arms thrash against the floor   her body convulsed beneath
stomach and hips   hair caught under one leg

"God. Now. Please."

She screams   Sappho screams   cunt driven from the floor
rising up   splitting open   clitoris hard   shadow whirls above
her legs   the knees dipped in light   the toes dipped in light
fingers sinking cruelly into hips   teeth and tongue clenched in
the flesh of a thigh   Celeste dives down past the morsel of the
clit   into the infinite opening of the cunt   tongue skewering
meat and body   into the juices of womanhood   the walls
squeezing in against her   crotch arching off the floor   hips
grinding into nose and face   eyes and cheeks coated now   the
reek as hot and heavy as hell   issuing from the cavern of the
womb   "Now." "Now." "Now." "Now." "Let me have it now."
Sappho cries   belly pressing between breasts   head pounding
again and again against the floor   hands spread-eagling legs
body braced with body   clit rasping against teeth   screaming
now   only with breath   cunt narrow   then slack   then narrow
then wide   then narrow   then loose   then tight   and tight and
tight   and grinding   and tight   and grinding   and tight   and
convulsively   with a great expellation of gas   coming   pleading

132

screaming gasping holding coming coming coming falling
exhausted back on the floor

The elevator sinking still below

it was almost
dawn when they reached the Sanctuary, but Killer was up,
sitting on the porch, writing in the rain.

He looked up, smiling, hair and moustache dripping.
"Sleep with me, Celeste?"

"Okay."

And they all went in to bed.

3.

When she awoke there was a man's arm across the middle of her back. She lay on her stomach, face burrowed between two pillows, one leg half off the bed. Out of the corner of her eye she could see the arm twist into the shoulder socket, and the pale expanse of his back. His face was turned away, breath slow, the dark hairs thick down ear and neck. The stubble of his beard gleamed in the under curve of his jaw. His skin was pale and rough, up to the neck, dark and seamed beyond that. An edge of sunlight, coming through the naked comer windows, lanced into her eyes.

She sighed and rolled carefully from front to side to hips, turning in the circle of his arm, but not disturbing it. The room was empty, except for the mattress and box springs they lay on. He had painted the wall behind them and the door a dead black; the walls with the comer windows with white and blue checks; and the wall by the bathroom was coated with a three dimensional plastic that spun when she moved her head. A faded prayer mat lay in the middle of the bare floor.

She fished a joint out of the neat pile of clothing by the bed, and lit it with his lighter, the pop of ignition unexpectedly loud. The smoke was cool and sweet, penetrating deep into the moist tissues of the lungs, easing into the body. They had not even talked when they had crawled into bed; they had undressed and he had kissed her, a quick, fond kiss. He had fallen asleep first; she had curled up around him, face pressed into his neck, and remembered nothing more.

Now she bent forward and blew a long plume of smoke at his face. His nose wrinkled and he made a faint protesting sound high in his throat, eyes tightening rather than open. She took another hit and held it, leaning closer and blowing into his ear. His arm hooked against her side and pulled as he rolled up and slid her under him. She looked up, laughing, into his sleep-heavy face.

"Bitch."

"I don't like being ignored."

"No one was ignoring you."

"No one was doing anything else to me, either."

"Your point," his eyes crinkled up in a smile, mystery gone in sunlight, strength remaining.

She touched his lips with hers, quickly, and tugged his hair. "Well, either get up or get to it. We haven't got all day."

"Haven't we?" he mocked, eyebrows lifted. "Then I'd better get up," he swung around and sat leaning back, one arm still around her, "I can't even fuck without coffee."

"'I thought the requirements were quite different."

His teeth flashed in a grimace. "I haven't had any complaints before."

"I haven't had any action."

He looked back at her. "You're in a fey mood today."

"Fey?"

"Strange, anyway."

"Yes, I guess I am, Killer."

The muscles of his shoulders bunched in a shrug. "I'm going down stairs a sec to get some coffee. Want some?"

"Bring me a Coke."

"Ugh," he said, and shuddered, kissing her and going out.

She waited until the door closed behind him and went over to the windows. The sky was clear, rinsed clean by rain. The great time-stained buildings of the old city and the gleaming monoliths of the new as sharp and unreal as a stereoscopic postcard. The louvers were shut against the night's storm, and she cranked them open, a cool sweet breeze moving over her breasts. Below, the wall stood in the puddle of its shadow; the sun was almost exactly overhead, it was close to noon.

She yawned and turned away, stomach cramped with a momentary nausea uneasiness. She leaned against the glass, bare shoulder on the chill pane, retching. The raw emptiness of her stomach heaved up, knotting against itself. Then it settled back into place, a little sore but steady.

There were half-a-dozen joss sticks in a cup by the bed and she took one out, lighting it on the end of her joint, the perfume spiraling up into the air. A thin mist of lotus blossoms settled in the room, and she stuck the end of the stick in the wire screen of a window, smoking and watching the people outside.

"Coke?"

Killer stood in the doorway, tall and thin and pale, moustache almost to his chin, a cup in one hand and a glass in the other. The tangled sweep of his hair stuck out at odd, slept-on angles like a battered mop. His hands, at the ends of those long, skinny arms, were huge, enfolding cup and glass.

"Coke," she agreed, taking it from him and sitting on the edge of the bed.

"Is there life before breakfast?" he said, taking a sip and making a face. "Shit, that's good."

She looked up at him, a shaggy poet groggy with sleep, and wondered what it would be like to wake up next to him every morning.

"I wrote another poem last night."

She looked down at her lap, the curling hairs of the pubis, and rubbed at the faint soreness in her stomach. "While I was out with Sappho?"

"While you were out with Sappho."

"You didn't mind?"

His eyes met hers. "That you were out with someone else?"

"That I was out with a woman."

"No."

"I wondered."

The individual hairs of his day's-growth beard were like the light struck points of swords.

"But you went."

"I wondered; but I didn't think you'd mind."

"I didn't."

Her free hand twisted across her thighs. "Not if you wrote another poem."

He laughed, "Am I that transparent?"

"Sometimes."

136

A veil seemed to fall across the cavern-pitted surface of his eyes, and he fumbled through a jacket pocket, pulling out a crumpled sheet of paper. He cleared his throat.

"*Celeste: a cycle*
(part the second)
Prolog
a gift
time spun
wrought
of memory
and vision
gold
and starlight
       I.
sometimes
I stand
in that darker
darkness
before
the burst of dawn
and think
of all the dawns
before
and after
and your light
seems
stronger then

       II.
you came
in answer
or in summons
I cannot tell
only that
all parts are whole
I all ways
straight
and the laughter

of your presence
all my answers
    III.
there comes
a time
of unity
when all things
frozen
are complete
and that sight
is
the answer
and the dawn
Epilog
in other words
    I love you."

The gaunt line of his mouth, stressed by hollow cheeks and skull-tight flesh, was still, his eyes were carefully neutral, looking into hers.

"Killer," she said, "I want you," and he pulled her down onto him.

His moustache rasped against her lip, the ' caught, stiff as needles, stabbing, his mouth rough and chapped, but gentle, the tongue tracing the outline of her lips. The palms of his hands stroked her back, the fingers working into muscle and spine, finding nerve after nerve, soothing each knotted tendon and each tightened vertebra, caressing flesh, tangling in the black veil of her hair, drawing her head backward, and his tongue set fire to her throat. She moaned and shook her head, the hair falling around his face, and he ran his fingers through it, brushing it aside, touching cheeks and ears and eyes and nose and brow and chin. His fingers ran across her lips and she kissed them, each one separately, sucking them into her mouth and licking the salty flesh taste from them. He laughed and bit her shoulder, neck and chin, kissing her again, tongue deep and quick in hers.

The hot shaft of his prick rose between her legs, nestling in the nerve center of her crotch, rubbing slightly against the lips of her vagina. She closed her thighs, squeezing them around it; it jerked once, twisting along the glass-smooth flesh. His hands met just below the nape of her neck, arms down her sides, and he hugged her, tighter and tighter, forcing the breath from her lungs, bending her ribs, imprinting her flesh with his, trying, almost succeeding, to break the interface between their bodies and merge together. She held on, fingernails cutting into his shoulders, tongue lost in the quick, silver heat of his mouth.

He let go, and she rolled off, beginning to kiss the flat man-nipples of his chest, hands moving down over his body, breath milling the black pubic hair at the root of his penis. One of his hands still soothed her back, reaching the muscles through the electric mesh-net barrier of her skin, and it trailed off down her hip and leg as she bent along the inside of his thigh, working out to the knee and back to the scrotum. Her tongue slid, glistening, over the wrinkled skin, up the trunk of his phallus, over the sensitive circumcised foreskin to the gaping crack at the top. He thrust up against her, and her lips parted to receive him, mouth closing on the length of the shaft, tongue still quick, embracing it.

"Ah, God," he cried, hands on her face, drawing her back up to him. She seemed to slide across his sweat slickened flesh and spread her legs out beyond his, twisting under him, and his prick came into her. She wanted it, had wanted it, had hoped that she would feel what she was feeling, every inch of his entry, the whole length of his shaft as the head forced its way in from the lips of her vagina, up, walls giving before it, to the seat of her womb, reaching there and holding a very brief moment before he withdrew it. Her vagina contracted when he went out and received him when he pushed in, she held her arms against his back and pressed her face to the hollow of his chin, teeth in his neck.

She had not expected to come and did not let herself become excited. Her fingers dug into his flesh, bracing her against the power of his hips, and her cunt reached up eagerly to meet his charge, but her mind was a million million miles away, watching and listening, but isolated. She wanted him to have now what he was having, taking with an expert's skill, each thrust of his prick a new and wondrous sensation, building, beyond the icy barrier of her body, a need and fire greater than she had ever felt. But she did not feel it, sensed it only dimly, in the vast distance of her flesh, and waited, patiently, loving, until he was spent.

Afterward, when they were dressing, she thought she could still feel the warmth of his come in her cunt.

"Celeste?"

"Yes," she pulled the sweater over her breasts and glanced at him.

"I studied chiropracty when I was younger; you know, spine and nerves," his voice trailed off.

"Yes, Killer, I know what it is."

"Well...." The muscles of his face were tight with strain.

"Go ahead."

His eyes slid over her shoulder and seemed to focus on the whirling three-dimensional wall beyond.

"You can learn a lot from the spine, you know."

Somewhere a fly buzzed vainly against a window pane.

"What is it, Killer?"

His moustache quirked in a lop-sided grin.

"Well, Celeste, I think you're pregnant."

She nodded. "I'd begun to think so."

He looked down at her, eyes hooded in shadow. "That makes a difference, doesn't it?"

Her fingers brushed his moustache down.

"Yes, darling. I'm afraid it does."

He grabbed her by the arms and jerked her to him, bending her head back until she stared at him.

"Celeste, what are you going to do?"

"That's up to me, isn't it?"

He let go and turned to look out the win, and his voice, when he answered, was as the echo of words spoken far away. "Yes, I guess it is."

She took his hand. "Then let's go down and join the others."

140

EPILOGUE
Redemption

A faint drizzle still fell across the city when the cab stopped. She looked up, out the window, at the house silhouetted against the gray evening sky. It was a wide building, bulky as a mountain, and the lights from its windows shone like jewels through the beads of water gathered on the panes. Down the slope of the hill, a swimming pool glimmered in a distant flash of lightning, and the wind blew across it, rippling the surface. Thunder shattered around them, and the driver turned, his face old and tired in the waxy light.

"This the place, lady?"

She nodded, reading the meter over the shoulder of his blue uniform. "Yes, thank you."

He folded the money in his meaty fingers. "Need any help?"

"No," she answered, wishing it were not quite so obvious.

He snorted, settling back down in the seat, "Just be careful going up those steps."

"All right," she slipped the strap of the bag over one shoulder and opened the door, bracing herself against the February wind. She had only worn a jacket, not expecting to need anything heavier, and the cold cut straight through to her bones.

There was a puddle under the door, and she stepped over it, the rain soaking instantly into her hair, and it clung, plastered, to shoulders and cheeks. She stood a moment, listening to the engine grind and then catch hold, a cool mist blowing across her lips. A leaf skittered along the pavement, lost in the dark, and she straightened her shoulders, going up slowly, step by step, using the handrail. The doctor had warned her to be careful, and she had already learned she could no longer trust her balance.

The doors were massive wood, oak, perhaps, and she pushed the button set between them, unable to hear anything inside the house. Lightning forked down the sky, and the lights in the windows flickered, going out. She huddled in the shadow of the porch, away from the wind.

It had been the only possible decision, but she wasn't sure it was the right one, and, wet and cold and miserable, belly aching, she regretted it more than ever, now, more, even, than when Killer had told her and she had made it. It seemed the last step of insanity down a road of madness, but it was what she wanted, and she clung to it, even here, in the wet and cold, far from them all. She shoved her hands into the pockets of her jacket and hugged her stomach, trying to ease the strain.

A short, pudgy man, eyes gleaming behind contacts, opened the door, a candle in one hand. "Yes?"

"Are you his butler?" she asked.

"No, I'm his business manager."

He stood in the crack of the door, shielding the interior with his body, not blocking it, but not letting her in, the guttering candle bright on his face.

"Can I come in?"

"Who shall I say is calling?" His stare was flat and level, the flame a pinpoint reflection in his pupils.

"His wife."

The skin of his eyes seemed to blink down, but his glare was unwavering. "His wife?"

"His wife," she repeated.

In his hand the candle trembled and the light swam over his face, over the line of his mouth, and he spoke in a whisper, "All right, come in. I'll give him your message."

He stepped back, and, in the darkness, she shrugged, following him down a wide entrance way, past shadowed paintings, to a table set with candles. The rain dripped from her hair, and she turned, mouth working into a bitter grin.

"Wait in there," he gestured briefly to a door. "I'll find him."

She took one of the candles and walked into the room. The walls, lined with books and video tapes, rose two stories to a stained glass ceiling; a video tape machine stood at the far end, under a painting. The painting seemed the focus of the room, hanging on a bar wall, high above the floor. She raised the candle and went toward it.

It was a painting of her face.

The light stained it with amber shadings, and the sound of her steps was lost in the depths of the carpet. The room was a mahogany and leather study done in books, the less pretentious volumes hidden behind leaded glass. Across the desk, the cushioned throne of his chair faced the video tape screen, and four stereo speakers were set above, one at each comer of the room.

She stopped under the painting, looking up. It had the flat perfection of a portrait done from a photograph. There was no way he could have a photo of her, and she leaned back against the desk, wondering.

Somewhere back east, Sappho and Killer were already married. She had brought them together, and if she had done nothing else with her life, she had accomplished that. Her hands rubbed her stomach, trying to work the soreness from the muscles; she had not wanted to think of them, leaving had been very difficult. They had spent three months together, living together, laughing together, loving together. She missed them. They were the first people she had ever really loved, and all the wild, aching nights they spent together had been worth it.

Andre Fuller had had a million sperm-drenched nights, a thousand lusting orgasms, an endless number of spent, bursting comes, and every one of them had been empty, every one guaranteed good. And, if this was the price she had to pay, if she were never to have another climax, then it was worth it, because every night for the last three months, she had been loved. And, if all the million blind, satiated nights had to be paid for, then she was willing to accept the price, for their love, and hers.

She smoothed the front of her skirt, remembering . . . remembering the contraceptive laden air of the dome . . . remembering the salty taste of the first driver's semen . . . remembering the friction of the second driver's rubber . . .

144

remembering that she had slept with no one else until Sappho . . . she was still standing there, remembering, when he came in.

"Celeste?"

The flame of the candle guttered as she whirled, and the flesh jerked tight against his face, as if, standing in the doorway, not moving, he were holding some great emotion under control, and, if he were to move, it would run berserk. His hand slowly loosened the collar of his velvet shirt, and dropped heavily to his side. In a moment his eyes lowered to her stomach, and, refocusing, but not shifting, came back to her face, and then her stomach, and then her face. And, very deliberately, his head came up, the glare of the candle bright in his eyes.

"Are you going to try and tell me it's mine?"

She looked at him, not daring to move her eyes, hip pressed against the side of the table, words firm and clear. "Yes, Howard, if you'll let me."

His voice did not shake, because he would not let it, but the words were strained with the effort. "Are you going to tell me that you've slept with no one else?"

"No, Howard. I'm not going to tell you that. It would be a lie. But I am going to tell you that it is yours, and that it can be proven if you want."

He reached into a pocket. "Is it money?"

The candle trembled in her hand, and wax spilled across her thumb. "No, I didn't come back because of money."

His flesh had gone white, but his voice was normal. "Then why are you here?"

"Because of you."

He laughed.

"I don't expect you to believe it," she whispered. "I don't expect you to believe that I care about you. I don't expect you to believe that I ran away because I did care about you; and I was frightened. I don't expect you to believe that I came back because I still care about you, and I'm not afraid anymore."

His face had grown as pale and smooth as carven alabaster, and he raised a hand, to speak, but she plunged on, harsh with strain, ' "But I can tell you why I think you married

145

me. Remember, you didn't think I'd understand, and I didn't. But I do now. Doesn't that mean I've changed? That's what I'm trying to tell you. I've changed. I want another chance. I don't deserve it. But I want it."

His lips, and the flesh around his eyes, were white, and a nerve jumped at the corner of his mouth, but she ignored him. "You saw fear and need in me, a terrible need to be cared for, and you wanted to answer that need. You were alone, and you understood loneliness, you wanted to reach me across it. You wanted me to reach you across it. You sensed that strange, almost innocent, passivity I had, and you wanted to understand it, knowing you could never truly break the barrier between 'I' and 'you' and really understand. But wanting to try anyway. You saw that I never wanted to hurt anyone again, and you had been hurt too often. I fascinated you."

She took a breath.

"Celeste."

"Shut up," she shouted. "Give me a chance, damn it." Her breath was sharp and painful. "I don't care if you don't believe me. Please, just take me on the same terms. Let me be an expensive whore, a permanent whore. Nothing more. I don't deserve anything more. Just give me that chance."

He looked at her, and he did not move, but through some subtlety of candlelight his face changed, softened, but she did not dare allow it to soften, and went on, "Only you have to know the truth about—"

"—I know the truth, Celeste," he glanced up at the painting, "the picture was from the television accounts of the trial. I discovered that later, when I was trying to find you. It explained a lot."

She sat the candle down on the edge of the desk; it fluttered and went out, a faint glow from the hall outlining him in the doorway.

"And?"

He sighed, "I love you."

He came to her . . . across the Formica table topped restaurant . . . across the courtroom . . . across the hospital cell .

. . across the motel room . . . across the acid-bent floor of the church . . . across the length of the continent . . . across the streets of New York . . . across the space of the room . . . across the space of her life . . . he came to her, and she closed her eyes in the darkness, pulling him with her to the softness of the carpet.

His body was hard and male in her arms, heavy and solid, and she held her lips to his, tongue moving in his mouth. He kissed back, fingers uncertainly charting the surface of her face. She grabbed his wrists, holding his palms against her cheeks, kissing the fingers, pressing herself against him. His tongue lanced between two fingers, sucking her lips into his teeth.

"Ahhh," she moaned, writhing under him, pressing her crotch against his leg, the friction running down the opening, into her womb, and bit him along throat and neck, peeling back his collar, a slow heat spreading through her loins. His hands slid over her body, touching breasts and the distorted mound of her belly. She reached up under his shirt, filling her senses with the smooth warmth of his skin.

His tongue invaded her breast, working down along blouse and jacket, her flesh aching beneath his mouth, an answering ache echoing in her womb. Her vagina knotted around itself, empty, closing on nothing, empty, needing to be filled, and she pulled the shirt up over his arms, rubbing her cheek over his bare chest, blowing on the flat nipples. He kissed her again, and she pressed up against him, his fingers unzipping jacket and blouse, releasing the bra, tracing the curves of her swollen breasts, spiraling in narrower and narrower circles toward the puckered teat.

She scraped her nails down his back and his fingers clenched in the nipple, the thumb rolling over it and hunger ate through her body. She held him, face cradled in his shoulder, clinging to the warm flesh, and let him push her back down, his mouth flicking across her nipple. "Yes," she said. "Yes."

He rocked back to his knees, and unbuckled the belt of her skirt, she raised her hips, and his fingers slid under it and her panties, tugging them down off her legs. She edged away from the wet clothing, closer to the bookcases, and he followed her,

147

his palms caressing her belly. He lay his face on it and looked at her between the slopes of her breasts. His eyes were wide and his breath came quietly.

After a while, still lying there, he ran a hand up the inside of her thigh to the crotch, his fingers moving through the slick, damp flesh, gently stroking it. She rested her hand on his face, closing her eyes again, sensing his finger as it hesitated, and plunged into the tunnel of her womb. It came past every inch of skin, and every convolution of flesh, and she tightened around it, her body relaxing, pressing against, pressing harder against it, the pressure stronger than his finger or her vagina, and fell back, spent, the pressure growing.

She was not afraid, merely tired, and she drew his face up to hers, tongue licking the salt from his eyelids, and he slid out of his pants, rolling gently on her, supporting his weight with his arms, easing onto her belly. There was no pain, no fear, only an enormous pressure from her throat to her hips, straining in the walls of her cunt, and, for a moment, as he entered, the pressure left, ahead of him, just ahead, but returned, down the length of his prick, and he touched bottom, reached the beginning of her womb, and her body strained against him.

He pulled out carefully, and thrust back in, carefully. His strokes were long and slow, almost hesitant, the pressure going and coming and building and growing until it became as steel in her muscles, and she held him to her, his prick moving in her cunt, sobbing on his chest, reaching out to meet him, body lost in blood-shot darkness, trying to meet him, trying to take him all the way in, trying to answer the tension of his body with the tension of hers, trying to take him all the way in until his final questions were answered, and the final mysteries revealed, trying to make of this one fuck, an honest fuck, trying to reach him and tell him, with her body, through her body, that she loved him, and, because she loved him, he could have her, any time, any day, any where, for any reason, to answer his needs and his love, and tell him . . . tell him . . . tell him . . . but the pressure in her gut was too great, and she could no longer think, only cling, and he drew out, slowly, slowly, the

148

flesh closing in after him, and thrust again, and again, and again, and again, and the pressure built and built and built until she hung on the brink of a precipice, and he slammed into her, and slammed, and slammed, and slammed, and she screamed, hanging, for a split second, on the edge, and fell, plummeting, into . . .

CLIMAX

AFTERWORD

"Who will speak out for the mad dreamers?

... There is no foundation that will enfranchise them, no philanthropist who will risk his hoard in the hands of the mad ones.

And so they go their ways, walking all the plastic paths filled with noise and neon, their bee-eyes seeing much more than the clattering groundlings will ever see, reporting back from within their torments that ... the midnight of madness is upon us, that wolves who turn into men are starving our babies, that trees will bleed and birds will speak in strange tongues....

The geniuses, the mad dreamers, those who speak of debauchery in the spirit, they are the condemned of our times; they give everything, receive nothing, and expect in their silliness to be spared the gleaming axe of the executioner....

The mad ones will persist. In the face of certain destruction they will still speak of the unreal, the forbidden, all the seasons of the witch.

Do not be misled: you have just read a novel. It is about The Season of the Witch."

Harlan Ellison

(Excerpt from Harlan Ellison's Afterword to the 1968 Essex House edition, written in an attempt, he stated elsewhere, to capture the flavor of "newness" he found in the book's style; revised into standalone form, this piece was next republished in Richard Geis' *SF Review* as "Black Thoughts/Blood Thoughts" and with additional afterthoughts was reworked for the *1983 Yearbook* of P.E.N. Los Angeles as "A Love Song for Jerry Falwell.")

To those who enjoyed this book as is, my sincere appreciation.

To those who were aware of its deficiencies, which loom ever larger to its author thirty-some years later, "my blushes," as a famous man once remarked to his life-long companion.

Today metaphors like "cinemascope" and "Formica," seem anything but futuristic. I knew too little to realize anything that had become omnipresent must be on its way out. The dialogue seems callow and pretentious, and the poetry ... ugh! But, if you liked it, I won't spoil your memories with any further self-denigration.

If sexual anatomy and biology seem to equal psychological destiny (i.e., if you have a vagina you will learn to like men) in this book, write it off to the paucity of information available at the time which compounded my own and the era's ignorance, plus the fact that I was deeply under the sway of Ayn Rand at the time (but, ah, that great rape scene on the burlap bag in the tunnels of the Grand Central Station with the trains thundering by!).

I think I thought you had to be heterosexual to be a real woman (but then so did everyone, even many dykes, and all the professional psychiatrists who determined who was and was not a valid candidate for sex change therapy). This misapprehension on my part is even stranger when you consider that when asked for a biography for a convention program book not long after *Season of the Witch* was published, I provided a whimsical one which included authoring the fictitious book, *I Was a Male Lesbian*. Like so many people, I discounted my own inner wisdom here, because I discounted myself.

Having lived in the trans, queer and lesbian communities for sometime, I know better about many things these days, of course.

As to the plot, as any male-to-female crossdresser or transsexual knows, "forced feminization" is to us what the bodice-ripper (where the heroine is raped by the hero for 500 pages and then marries him and lives happily ever after) is to many women-born-women. And for the same reasons: "I want

152

it. It is forbidden. But if I was forced to do it, no one could blame me (and I could secretly enjoy it)." Such is the stuff of rationalization built of. As I said once in a speech, it is all one long masturbatory wet dream (to which the late Robert Bloch, author of *Psycho*, immediately quipped, "I had a dry dream once, but that turned out to be *Dune!*").

Oh well, let me admit to an unselfish motive. It was as clear to me in junior high school in 1958 Davenport, Iowa, that the girls among my peers were not treated or seen as human beings, in short, were victimized by their boyfriends, etc., as it is clear to everyone now. Thus the dedication to two important women in my life, in the hope that the treatment of women in society might someday be improved. That, at least, has happened to some degree and we will not argue about degree.

In short, for all its seeming lack of feminism at the start of the third millennium, the book was consciously intended to be feminist – then. Consider it ur-feminist and let it go at that.

As for what seems my singular failure to envision the future, I have no excuse. I guess I was concentrating too much on the experience of being in a woman's body, and writing too quickly to deadline, to realize this defect at the time.

I could also tell you about the derivation of names, I suppose. How "Josette" came from *Dark Shadows*, "Andre" had always struck me as cool, "Monkton" from the middle name of the villain in *The Fountainhead*, "Munger" was an entrepreneur I worked for who later produced a movie about the jail-cell spiritual conversion of one of the Watergate conspirators. Etc. But, what would it profit either of us? ("Sappho" indeed! I blush at the seeming crudity today.)

I should also mention that while watching an episode of the original *Star Trek* television show, and discussing the book with my partner, Frankie Hill (who was giving the text of this electronic edition a final proofreading), I remembered that Howard Sladek (probably from the character Howard Roark and the writer John Sladek) was based, in part, on my impressions of the Great Bird of the Galaxy, Gene Roddenberry, for whom I worked on developing the germ of a movie idea that, years later in other hands, became *Greystoke: The Legend of Tarzan.*

I suppose I owe you a few words about the prose. It was this way, I was high on mescaline, and – after seeking some advice from my friend, the science fiction critic William Glass, who referred me to the opening passages of Ted Sturgeon's *More than Human*, where he thought I might find a treatment of the kind of opening scene I wanted to write – I popped on a set of headphones, dropped something suitable on a turntable, and this trio of influences catalyzed into "stone flowers blossoming on the bone trellis of your skull."

As for the titles of the various parts, I confess I owe my inspiration to that giant among American women writers, Francis Parkinson Keyes, who, despite Harlan Ellison's suggestion in several speeches and articles, is not a purveyor of saccharine romance, but a seriously committed woman novelist. Her heroine in one book spends 250+ pages in the more primitive portions of 1930s South America while suffering from severe morning sickness, and 500 pages later, at the end, when her husband, is being presented as U.S. Ambassador to the Court of St James, lies through her teeth when he asks her and reassures him, "It was all worth it." (That's not what I call saccharine.) Although Keyes' *Also the Hills* simply put me away then, as it does now, it is to her *Steamboat Gothic* – and the way the titles of that book's five parts reflect the hero's moral lapse in pursuit of his goal, and the ultimate cost to him and later generations of his family – that I chose to emulate in mine.

Finally, it is clear to me in retrospect that, while I was instinctively on the mark in wanting to take the book's title from the Donovan song I was so infatuated with at the time, I chose the wrong phrase. Rather than having called this book *Season of the Witch* – which is so misleading in hindsight, and at most conjures some similitude of the feeling of the prose, of, if you will, the "dawning of the age of Aquarius" – the title I should have used, which would have captured the book's theme perfectly, is to be found in the Donovan lines that close the book. Alas! It was only in 1999, on millennial eve, that I realized that the ideal title, which had been staring me in the face for oh so long, was *Dark Princess*. Boo hoo! Just consider how redolent of the book's theme the following phrase would have been. "Do not be misled: you have just read a novel. It is about a Dark Princess."

In my own behalf, I should probably confess to an even greater blunder, titlewise. My original title was "The Place of Excrement" from the line in Yeats' poem, "Crazy Jane Talks with the Bishop," which reads, "love has pitched his mansion in the place of excrement," which encompassed many of the book's concerns about our negative mental associations with genitalia and sex. My editor, Brian Kirby, about whose genius so much has already been written – and still not one-half what he deserves – thought more wisely of the matter and suggested I seek a title somewhat less likely to turn readers off before they even picked the book up (with its suggestion that the book would be about coprophilia).

There is perhaps a last comment I should make re: the book, and this brings us to the heart ... well ... of my heart. No one can ever know what lonely, suffocating darkness those of us born transgender lived in during the late 1950s and early 60s. To my fourteen year-old self, the 1959 Billy Wilder movie, *Some Like It Hot*, was like a ray of light from God/dess above. The final scene and final line offered the only hope my sisters and I were to know for many years. (I can't believe there is anyone alive who is reading what I am writing here who has not seen this movie – but if you haven't, rent it tonight! When it's over, imagine you are me then and hear Joe E. Brown's final line being said lovingly to you personally! You will know how my heart leaped and how I wanted to leap on the screen and be the person next to him on the boat.) After finishing *Season of the Witch*'s final chapter recently, a friend remarked, "So it all comes down to 'nobody's perfect'?" The degree of progress TG people have made in the last thirty years might be seen in this: At the time I wrote the book, that level of acceptance and love was all I (or any trans person) could hope for – today, I hope for (and have) a whole lot more!

If you have primarily tuned-in because of the film version, *Synapse* (U.K. title, *Memory Run*), I must, first of all, give all credit where it is due, to the film's true, though uncredited, producer and credited screenwriter, David Gottlieb. It was David who single-handedly championed the transforming of the book into a movie for more than a quarter of a century (taking time out to produce and write other motion pictures and telefilms along the way), from the novel's original publication in 1968 until the commencement of production in Toronto in 1995. As for having the hero/heroine end up pregnant by himself, credit for that goes not to the book's author, who overlooked the possibility entirely, and solely to the film's director and script polisher, Allan Goldstein and Dale Hildebrand.

All told, except for the glaring need for some kind of lesbian sex scene, where the character would naturally continue to relate sexually to women as he always did, I am happy with the filmic result. They made the changes I would have made to exteriorize the theme of what is, after all, a stream-of-consciousness novel, and for me the essential theme of the mutability of gender is carried through to the end with the shot of Andre/now Josette standing with her baby and husband against the sunset – a shot that would be veritable cliché, if it were not for the fact that the woman in this bucolic trio was a man 90 minutes earlier in screen time!

Jean Marie Stine
July 4, 2000

Since writing the above, I have reread some of the glowing reviews, and those which claim *Season of the Witch* "depicts with painful accuracy how women are victimized in ... sexual encounters with men" and that it "reveals the exploitative and brutal secret life of America," do strike a familiar note. That is certainly what I was trying to capture at the time. Today my failures in that regard seem all too apparent. Perhaps I came closer to the mark then than I can realize today – or could realize then, when it seemed a much less blemished work of art in its author's eyes.

FILMOGRAPHY

Season of the Witch was filmed in Canada in 1996, with a U.S. release title of "Synape" and a European release title of "Memory Run." (I suggested "Thanks for the Mammaries" but was voted down.) The screenplay was by Allan Goldstein, David Gottlieb (II), Dale Hildebrand. The film was produced by Andy Emilio, Dale Hildebrand, and Walter Josten. The Director was Allan Goldstein. The true, uncredited producer was David Gottleib, who first optioned the film for production from me in 1969, kept pitching it for twenty-five years, secured development deals with various studios and production companies over the years, and suffered through endless rewrites of the script to suit many different producers' and directors' vision of the storyline, including one memorable incarnation that involved "betting for bodies"! The film involved funding from two production companies, a releasing company, and a patchwork of advance foreign rights sold - the total budget resulting from all these transactions, $1,300.000.

The cast included:
Karen Duffy as Celeste/Josette
Saul Rubinek as Dr. Munger
Matt McCoy as Gabriel
Lynne Cormack as Dr. Merain
Torri Higginson as Kristen
Barry Morse as Bradden
Chris Makepeace as Andre Fuller

Production credits included:
Cinematography by Curtis Petersen

Music by Varouje
Production Design by Ian Hall
Costume Design by Nancy McHugh
Film Editing by Evan Landis

At release it was 89 minutes and rated R for strong violence, sexuality and language.